YOUR
HONOR

Editor: Lisa Loewen
Cover Design: Sommer Stein of Perfect Pear Creative Covers
Formatting: CP Smith
Proof Readers: Amber, Lisa, Tera, Jamie, Ketty and Clista

PROLOGUE

Jenner

Professional Code of Ethics: Canon 3E/Rule 2.11(A) –Disqualification may be required if a judge's impartiality might reasonably be questioned if –Presiding over cases involving an attorney with whom the judge had a romantic relationship.

I read the Canon repeatedly, over and over again then chanted it to myself before I'd enter the courtroom. My entire life and career could potentially be at risk. Yet, seeing her crumbled every ounce of my resolve. Professionally, the control was mine as the judge. Personally, I choked on my words when it came to her. I didn't break easy but every time I saw her sitting in my courtroom as her beautiful lashes splayed over her eyes, I realized I didn't have a prayer. No matter which road I took, I had everything to lose.

CHAPTER 1

DISCOVERY

Lucy

"Cheers!" our group toasted in unison holding the shot glasses in the air. Supposedly, the creamy liquid was going to taste like Cinnamon Toast Crunch. Yes, the cereal, or so they said. Most shots were supposed to taste like some sort of concoction, yet for me, they tasted like gasoline scorching my throat.

For the past two years, I hadn't partied. I hadn't even had a drink. I'd barely left my apartment. Law school navigated my life, and in seven days I was starting my new job as an assistant district attorney in New York County. So tonight, we celebrated. I tossed the liquor into my mouth, I swallowed quickly hoping to avoid the awful taste.

"That wasn't too bad," Henley laughed, sliding her shot glass across the table.

I quickly glanced away as the flavor of Cinnamon Toast Crunch overwhelmed my taste buds.

Henley and I both gasped. "Oh. My. God! Cinnamon Toast Crunch!" We laughed and ordered two more.

"Hey, Lucy, these cupcakes are de-lish!" Kak said, filling her mouth with another bite.

"Thanks!" I replied. "My neighbor across the hall is a fantastic baker, and she's just getting started, so I peddle her name out whenever I can."

"They are decorated so cute."

I made a mental note to tell Midge the compliments about the cupcakes.

The music from the other room grew louder as the night grew later. Our private party in the back room was symbolic of what would happen to our graduating class or at least our group. Some of us ventured out into the big room to meet other people, drink more and possibly dance. Others stayed in their comfort zone of the back room with familiar faces. Inevitably, the party would be over and our friendships too would likely fade. Sad really.

Henley and I, however, would undoubtedly be a forever thing. Four years of college. Three years of law school. We had endured her series of monogamous relationships and my unwillingness to date let alone dive into a serious relationship.

"Well?" she asked as we stood in the doorway of the club. A group of men sat around a bar table in the corner by us. One hot guy in particular glanced my way. I'd sort of forgotten how to do this flirting thing as I awkwardly looked away. I'd never been a flirter. My mother had done enough for both of us.

"Well what," I asked, feeling the hot guy's eyes on me.

"Have you picked him out yet?"

"Stop."

"I am *not* going to stop. It's time," she said way louder than necessary. "Whatever lucky soul you pick is going to have to Indiana Jones that pussy. Those cobwebs are a force to be reckoned with." The music just happened to transition from one song to the next during her not-so-subtle declaration, and the guys from the corner overheard, turning in unison to look at us. Blood crept into my cheeks.

"Indiana Jones that pussy? Really? You're disgusting." I swatted at her, crinkling up my nose.

"And please, for the love of God, tell me you waxed or shaved like I suggested. We certainly don't want Welcome to the Jungle blaring out as you drop your panties."

Laughter erupted from the guys in the corner at that remark, and when I glanced at them, the hot, older guy winked at me. I offered him the fakest of smiles, bowed and curtsied in their direction, then flipped around to my obnoxiously crude friend.

"Thank you for that," I gritted, glaring at Henley.

She giggled, and then jerked my arm out of socket as she winked back at the table of guys and lugged me in the opposite direction.

"Whoever you finally give it up for after twenty-four years of no sex, he better be special or at the very least, memorable."

I smiled and glanced back at the guy with the dark eyes.

The farther we walked, the louder the music revved up. Girls in skimpy clothes gyrated around the dance floor, grinding on guys and other girls—flipping their hair all around. Some girls bent over touching their toes while guys grinded on their asses. Damn, I really needed to get out more.

I glanced down at my attire. Black fitted dress slacks. Collared dress shirt. It wasn't bad. It wasn't skanky. It didn't shout 'fuck me' from the ceiling. It didn't really shout anything though. Except maybe pussy cobwebs down below...

Jacque covered Henley's eyes from behind. He'd been crazy about her for the past year, but she wouldn't do it. His father was a tenth circuit judge and everyone knew that Jacque would do great things. Henley wanted to shine on her own. And one thing was for damned certain; she wouldn't be outshined.

Henley twirled around and began dancing with Jacque. Her clothes were fun, flirty. After glancing down at my humdrum outfit, I shook off my own doubt and strolled to the restroom. The bright lights of the bathroom never did anyone justice, but when I laid eyes on the cute, scarcely dressed girls by the sink, I wanted to punch myself for dressing the way I did. It stemmed from my mother. Because of her fire engine red lipstick, I barely wore any make-up. I dressed conservatively because she didn't and was always a cloud of embarrassment. She spent her time spreading her perfectly shaped legs for almost anyone, I'd sworn myself to a sexless life...until now.

Frustrated, I hit the door of a stall, laying a paper toilet seat cover over the seat and sitting.

My brain was foggy from the earlier shots and drinks; I stood, finding drunken courage that I normally wouldn't have; I unbuttoned the top button of my dress shirt and the bottom three. After fastening my dress slacks, I tied the bottom of my shirt in a knot, allowing my belly button to show, flushed the toilet, washed my hands and strolled right back out into the club. I might be a nerdy little attorney but I could sexy this shit up real fast.

From the bar, I watched Henley and Jacque grooving away. They really would make the perfect couple.

"What can I get you?" the bartender asked, cupping his hand around his ear to capture what I requested.

"Um. How about a martini." I didn't drink enough to have a preferred drink of my own.

"Ok. What kind?"

I shrugged. "Never had one. Nothing sweet."

He tossed a cocktail napkin in front of me. "Ok. Gin or Vodka."

"Gin, for me," a deep voice behind me said. "Dirty."

"What's dirty mean?" I asked the man whose dark eyes I'd locked with earlier at the back table. The brighter light over by the bar did him justice. Flirt, I thought to myself. As casually as I could, I glanced at his ring finger, no ring. This was him...Indiana Jones...I could feel my skin tingle.

"Make her a dirty vodka. Put it on my tab," he instructed.

Ding. Ding. Ding. Bonus. He bought me a drink. "I know I'm just throwing it out there but would you want to have sex with me tonight? Like a no strings attached sort of thing," I blurted out immediately.

The bartender chuckled. "Wow," he said sliding the full martini glass my way. "Please tell me you two know each other." He raised his brows at the man I'd just propositioned.

"Nope. Haven't really even met."

The bartender stared at me for a long second. "That was slick," he added as he walked away shaking his head.

Wanting to magically disappear, I took a sip out of the fancy glass; the saltiness of the drink surprised me, and when I glanced up, the guy, who grew hotter by the sip, was staring at me.

"Sorry," I said.

"Sorry for what?"

"Blurting that out. What can I say? This girl's got game." I grinned.

"I see nothing wrong with being upfront and honest."

After a big gulp and devouring an olive, I shrugged. "I know you heard the cobwebs remark. So, it's whatever."

He shook his head of slightly gelled, brown hair. Well-shaped sideburns came down the side of his handsome face. "It was actually the Welcome to the Jungle comment that sealed the deal." When he smiled, his entire face lit up.

"Are you gay?" I spat out, wondering why he hadn't jumped at the chance of unobligated sex? Wouldn't most guys?

He didn't answer, only rolled his eyes and took another long drink.

"It's ok if you are. I'm not saying that being gay is bad. It's just..." I decided to quit while I was ahead, though I didn't feel ahead.

The conversation sort of took an awkward turn after that. Self-doubt reared its ugly head as I began to gnaw on my bottom lip. I had asked a guy to have sex with me and gotten no response. Perfect. My confidence plummeted.

Pulling his hand from his pants pocket, his thumb freed my lip from my teeth. God, it had been so long. Just his finger touching my lip caused everything inside of me to tighten.

"What makes you think we should sleep together?"

"You mean besides the Temple of Doom sort of comment," I laughed as the vodka began to swim freely through my veins. "And seriously, you need to be attracted to someone in order to even get it up, so if you're not attracted me, that's fine."

"Getting it up isn't a problem."

"Honestly, it's ok. In fact, the next guy that walks up to this bar, I'm going to ask him to have sex, and if he says yes, you are out of luck, buddy. You sat on answering way too long," I teased.

I drew a hint of blood this time as I bit down on the same part of my lip. It had been a habit for as long as I could remember. Typically, I switched sides so the same spot didn't get too raw. Once again, his thumb freed my lip from my destructive teeth, but this time his thumb brushed gently over my entire bottom lip and gave me a shit-eating grin.

"You're beautiful. You don't need me to tell you that. But, I must say, you are especially stunning now that you tied your blouse in a knot."

He winked, a bucketful of butterflies tipped over in my stomach even though he was totally making fun of me.

"I know. Lame attempt with fitting in." I shot back the martini—which I quickly learned was not a shooter on any level. Involuntarily, I blew out my now salty, dragon breath. "My God," I whispered.

"Fit in with who?"

I motioned toward the dance floor. "Them. The Barbies trying to land Ken. You know, the skanks and ho bags."

He chuckled, exposing perfectly aligned, white teeth.

"It sounds like you're setting your sights high…are you shooting to be a skank or a ho?"

"Ho *bag*," I corrected, swatting my hand at him. I rolled my eyes. "You know what I mean."

"Is that why you asked me to have sex with you?"

When I glanced at him, his brown eyes seared into me making me nervous. There was something demanding about him…yet gentlemanly. A professional aura that rang out through his clothes and shoes.

"No," I whispered, suddenly embarrassed of my request for sex. "That pretty much shouted skank though, huh?"

"You are clearly not a skank," he said finishing his own drink.

It only took a second or two this time for me to stop chewing on my lip…well; it actually took his hand moving toward my mouth again for me to stop. His hand redirected, going in a different direction; his fingers intertwined with mine.

"And your offer still stands?"

"Hey!" a guy shouted as he stepped up to the bar. "Can I get two jagerbombs and two slippery nipples!" The size of his nose ring was larger than any I'd seen. My eyes widened.

The guy I'd been chatting with arched his brows and tilted his head toward nose ring guy. I'm guessing he was remembering my threat to ask the next guy at the bar to have sex.

I shook my head, grinning, then mouthed no.

"Let's get back to your offer. Does it still stand?"

My swallow got stuck somewhere in my throat.

"My offer?" my voice shot up in shock as I realized this might really happen.

The most perfect slight smile touched his lips as he tilted his head—a silent reminder.

"Oh, sex?" I nearly shouted. "Yep! Offer still stands."

The bartender glanced at us again, giving me a mocking thumbs up.

"Perfect. I'll tab out, tell my friends I'm leaving and meet you at the door."

As his stool scooted away from the bar, I grabbed his hand. "Wait, what's your number?"

His dark eyebrows met in the middle. "My number? Why?"

Shrugging, I said, "Look at this place. It's huge. I just thought I'd text when I got outside."

His eyes scanned the massive crowd but he still looked at me with hesitation… skepticism. I quickly shook my head, warding off his look of concern.

"I just meant in case we got separated. I wouldn't text you after if that's your concern. I'd never do that. You'll never hear from me again. I told you no strings attached. But for tonight, you're committed." I winked.

The darkness in his eyes was somewhat intimidating but seemed to soften with my poor attempt at humor. As I took a step back, his gaze searched my face for something, maybe honesty. His tongue peaked out between his lips.

"641-913-"

As quickly as possible I typed in his number so I could text him after telling Henley goodbye. He spat out the last four numbers so quickly, I wasn't sure I'd gotten them right but didn't want to make him repeat himself.

When I looked up from my phone, the vodka had gotten the best of my brain cells, and I accidentally stumbled into him.

"Did you drive?" he asked, helping me find my balance. There was a seriousness in his tone that sobered me a little. I knew nothing about the man I was leaving a club with. This had missing woman all over it. I could be on a milk carton by morning.

"Sorry," I whispered, backing up. "No. I wouldn't drink and drive. But seriously, I am a drink away from slobbering drunk."

He chuckled and then turned and strolled toward his friends.

Quickly, I found Henley and whispered that I was leaving with the hot guy from earlier. She immediately shot a stare back at the table where the guys had been earlier, clearly searching for him. When I pinched her arm, she jerked away laughing.

"I want to see him!" she shouted.

"I'll text you tomorrow."

"Text me tonight! I want to know someone finally broke on through to the other side." She knew I hated Jim Morrison.

I nodded. "If I wind up dead…"

She hugged me. "You're not going to be dead. He was with an entire of group of professionals. But text me, ok?"

I took a deep breath ready for my night with Mr. Unknown. I glanced around, looking for him, but didn't see him. I liked him enough already that I hoped he hadn't bailed. I liked him enough already? Good conversation does not a relationship make.

The cool air was refreshing as I dashed toward the restroom to pee and freshen up, nerves suddenly getting the better part of me. A little uncertain, I texted his number:

Hey. This is me. That way you don't lose me. ☺

Outside, the air wasn't as cool, but the wind whipped my hair in my face. He, whatever his name was, wasn't out there and he hadn't texted back. I didn't know his name. This was exactly something Pops would be angry about. My pops would have wanted his ID, his driver's license number, phone number and social security number. The only number I had for him—he wasn't responding to. And on a scale from one to ten… Mr. Martini was a 10.

A blacked out Audi pulled to a stop in front of me. The tinted window lowered and there he was—Mr. Fuck Me Tonight. When he smiled, my stomach turned over. He was way sexier than anyone I knew. Out of habit, I bit my lip, until his eyes narrowed playfully; I smiled so goofily

I couldn't bite it if I wanted to.

He started to get out of the car, and I hustled to the passenger side door before he could.

"This isn't a date. Let's not make it more than it is," I said teasingly as I slid into the car.

The smell…his smell… swallowed me. A mixture of new car and sexy man teased my nose and an unfamiliar, tingling sensation flitted between my legs. Unintentionally, I arched my hips up.

"Everything ok?" he asked with a cocked brow.

I nodded. "Yes. It's just a been a while and I think my body is ahead of my mind."

"Why has it been a while? You're a stunning girl."

I didn't like lying. When I noticed the sunroof, I pushed the button, exposing the sky.

"I had some things I needed to take care of first. I think we should have sex under the stars," I suggested, relaxing my head on the headrest and staring at the white-sparkly, dark sky.

"Do you now," he chuckled, shooting a U-turn in the middle of the road.

"Wrong turn?"

"Just an idea."

Inhaling a deep breath, I hoped tonight was earth shattering in a non serial killer sort of way. After a few minutes, we darted into a parking garage. He parked, unlocked the doors and got out.

"Come on."

I followed, and though he stayed right next to me, we didn't really say much. The frosted-glass, automatic doors opened, exposing a Waldorf logo.

He brought me to a hotel? A freakishly nice one, but still… It was at least safe.

"Scared to take me to your house, eh?" I asked with a hint of playfulness.

"No. Wait here."

My eyes followed him as he walked over to the front desk area. His body filled out his clothes nicely. My lids grew heavy as I waited, my head spun—one of the worsts side effects of alcohol. I couldn't help but wonder if this was an alcohol induced decision… of course it was. So what, I needed to live a little.

"Second thoughts?" he asked, stirring me from my drunken, turned-on stupor.

"Negative." I shot upright, wavering once again on my feet. The strength in his hands forced another cringe of tightening deep in my pelvis.

The heated tension between us in the elevator choked me, and my lips parted trying to catch my breath. I'd never given myself the opportunity to feel this…this desire with any man. I fought so hard not to follow in my mother's footsteps that I'd abandoned that basic need and desire found inside all of us. When I tried to catch a glimpse of him peripherally, I realized how tall he actually was.

The tip of his tongue greeted my glance as he moistened his lips, and a smile nipped at the corners of my lips. He was going to kiss me, I thought. My heart pounded in my throat and my thoughts were fuzzy. Downing that martini in a single swig may not have been the best idea. He didn't kiss me.

The ritzy suite was luxuriously chilly and a subtle shiver fluttered up my spine just as his hand rested at the small of my back. Coincidence?

"Would you like a drink?" he asked.

"No, thank you," I whispered slowly, taking in the enormity of the suite. The bed was massive. I swallowed the reservations that crept up my spine and found him sitting on the arm of the sofa watching my every move.

"You know, you could kill me and no one would be the wiser."

A gentle grin touched his lips. "Outside of our friends, the bartender, the guy at the front desk and every camera between here and there, you mean? Plus, they would discover where your cell phone pinged over the past few hours and oddly enough, mine would have pinged off the same towers. Then there is the little text that you sent. What was it you said?" He tilted his head to the side. "'Hey. This is me. That way you don't lose me.' Did I get that right?"

"You didn't respond."

"I don't text."

I spun around, my mouth gaping. "You do too."

He shook his head, sliding his hands into his pockets. "No. I don't."

"That's because you're worried I'll creep on you when we are done."

"It's not just you. I don't text anyone," he explained.

"Why?"

He shrugged. "Not a fan."

"Well, I'm sure tonight will be so good that those little thumbs of yours will be texting away…chasing me as I walk." My own words forced me to smile.

His knees cracked as he got to his feet. He didn't seem *that* old. Heat spread through my lower half as he gradually made his way to me. "There are two things I don't chase, liquor and beautiful women. Besides, I specifically recall a no strings attached stipulation." He stopped, leaving about 12 inches between us.

"Trust me, when I give anything, including myself, it doesn't come with strings."

I wanted to know what he was thinking as his eyes darted back and forth between my eyes and my mouth.

Trying to break the ice, I kicked off my shoes and glanced toward the bed. "Well, since you can't kill me…" I winked at him and tilted my head toward the bed.

His eyes darkened as he unbuttoned the cuffs on his dress shirt.

"Are we gonna exchange names?" I asked.

When his jaw ticked from a firm clench, I guessed that was a no.

"It's ok." For some unexplainable reason, I wanted to make him feel better about not telling me his name. "We could make up names, if that makes you more comfortable."

A low part-grumble part-chuckle worked its way through his chest.

"And, what would your name be?" he grinned, exposing a white t-shirt beneath his navy and white checked shirt that he hung over a chair.

This suddenly seemed awkward…forced… as we both undressed… ourselves. "Monica?" I asked.

"Friends?"

I nodded. I honestly loved Monica.

"Fine. Then, I'll go with Richard."

I shoved him backward. "No way!" I shouted just like Monica would. "Tom Selleck was so freaking hot in that role."

"Then, I'm perfect." His mouth pulled into a lopsided grin.

He really was perfect. My slacks pooled around my feet, and in his t-shirt, with his jeans unfastened, he finished his stroll toward me. Muscles were way more visible now that he was only in his undershirt—a different sexiness than I'd seen earlier. My heart pounded in the back of my throat as he reached for the buttons on my shirt. What the hell, this was really going to happen. I'd never done anything like this in my entire disciplined life.

Once my blouse fell to the floor, his lips brushed over my shoulder, sending a flurry of goose bumps fanning out over my skin. He and I still hadn't kissed. Maybe that was better. A kiss was so personal.

I didn't realize his hands were near my bra, but when I felt the coolness of the air pebble up my nipples, I gasped. I watched as he deftly navigated my straps off my shoulders, letting the bra fall freely to the ground. My God. My body hummed with desire.

The back of his fingers grazed over my nipples and it was agonizingly pleasurable. A slight moan crept up my throat. Even though his lips didn't touch mine, his eyes kissed every inch of me.

"You like that?" he asked as two of his fingers lightly squeezed my nipples.

"Yes."

He turned me around toward the cushioned bench sitting at the end of the bed. "Sit."

I did, without thinking about what he was even asking. There was something about him that demanded compliance. I watched him unbutton his pants and remove them, leaving only his boxer briefs on, which had a noticeable bulge. After creasing the pants, he folded them over a chair as well. His OCD tendencies were obvious.

In law school, I had learned to maintain a poker face, to not show my hand. I fought any reaction to the enticing bulge or to the mystery between us.

"Stand up. Please." He added the please after I'd already begun to stand, and then he took the seat I had just vacated. He took my hand in his, pulling me toward him.

Before I could say a word, his fingertips grazed over the lace on my panties. Panties that Henley and I had carefully selected for exactly this monumental moment earlier in the evening.

"Sit," he said again. He meant on him?

"Like on…"

He lifted my leg, placing one foot on one side of him and the other foot on his other side—straddling him.

I nestled down rubbing myself against his bulge, trying to act like I knew what I was doing. As if I had experience…as if. The darkness in his hooded and lust-filled eyes was seductive as hell. I wondered what he saw in mine.

I sat above him, my breasts near his mouth. When he leaned forward, I instinctively arched toward him. The anticipation of his mouth drove me insane. I wanted him to touch me, to taste me.

The warmness of his mouth…of his tongue… the way he knew to swirl around my nipple. The feel of his hands as he palmed and massaged my breast. Oh. My. God. I'd never felt anything like this. A fuel lived within his tongue that lit a fire inside me. My hips began to work back and forth trying to create friction between us.

When his arms snaked around my waist, securing me tightly next to him, a small gasp fled my lips. In a matter of three seconds, he lifted me, rotated us around and laid me flat against the bed, all while continuing to savor my breasts. I swore in my head I wouldn't stop him. Ever.

But, then he stopped…I could tell my panties were wet. Drenched. I felt embarrassed at what little it took for my body to be completely ready for him. He began to work his way down my abdomen. He didn't know me, and I was surprised he would go down on me, but who the hell was I to stop him.

"You don't have to do that," I whispered.

"Please," he said with a low growl. "I already hear Axel and Slash cueing up."

I smiled as his fingers broke the barrier of my panties. Thank God, I had shaved per Henley's encouragement.

"You're a liar. There's no jungle," he said with playfulness in his tone. Then in a single swift movement, his finger slid effortlessly through my wetness and penetrated me. He pushed my knees apart with his other hand.

"Mmm," I hummed quietly as another finger joined the first.

"Mmm, is a perfect description," he whispered.

But I swear to God on my future children's lives—the feeling when his thumb began its perfect, circular assault, was the bomb that ricocheted anticipation tremors through my body. My hips arched to meet his touch. His mouth lowered over my breast and the mixture… My. God. The mixture of the unknown, the pleasure of the two-finger penetration, his thumb rotation, the soft swirl around my nipple. My God!

"I'm…" I wanted to articulate in some way that I was going to come. That it took only a minute or two to get me there. That I was going to explode by the hands of an actual man and I couldn't even form the words to say it. This was happening so much faster than it ever had for me. T -10 seconds until detonation.

"Please, do," he groaned, reading my mind. Then his mouth lowered over my breast again and with one swirl of the nipple…my lord…my uterus swirled into this century with an explosion of epic proportions. Pulse after pulse of contractions.

"Ahhh…." I moaned, and when I opened my eyes, his were above mine watching me. If any blood could have crept into my face, it would have.

"Sweet Jesus."

His words surprised me. He hadn't come, I had. I chuckled uncomfortably.

"Welcome back to the world as it should be," he added. "Why the time away?"

"School," I panted, lying again, sort of, and trying to catch my breath as his two fingers pulled out of me.

"Fair enough. I understand that. Come here for a minute." He stood, pulling me to my feet before guiding me out two French doors onto a balcony. My legs barely held my weight without buckling.

"Oh, my goodness," I said as I gazed out over the amazing New York skyline. The skyline I loved. "Richard. This is beautiful." The night air had cooled a bit especially to a naked, overheated body.

"Don't call me Richard. My name is Jenner."

I grinned.

"I brought you to the hotel because you mentioned having sex under the stars. I've stayed here, in the penthouse before, and this balcony patio is perfect."

The penthouse... My goofy grin turned into a full-blown smile. "Thank you." It was as if he knew this was an epic moment in my life too.

I forced my head to stop overthinking what this was. Even if he had done something incredibly nice and even though he was freaking hot and even though he was being respectful and kind and seemed utterly perfect...this meant nothing.

Two lounge chairs with thick, padded cushions sat in a corner on the balcony. Trying to take the lead, I walked toward them. I bit down on my lip where he couldn't see as I laid down on one of them. Under the stars...

I could feel my nipples harden without even looking at them. The wetness between my legs was cooled by the wind.

"And your name is?" he asked.

"Lucy. And please, no Charlie Brown jokes."

His smile was beautiful as he shook his head. "I never would have thought of Charlie Brown. Lucille Ball is the only real Lucy."

I put up a leg blocking him from coming any closer. "I beg your pardon. Though, I *was* named after her because of the red hair. The real Lucy is right here, baby." I teased with a smile.

Why did I want him to like me so much?

"I'm going to nail Lucy as soon as she stops talking about things like Charlie Brown."

"Whah whah whah whah." I mimicked Charlie Brown's teacher.

He laughed as he got closer, and I decided I couldn't wait for him to nail Lucy.

A phone rang from the other room, and his brow pulled together. His entire posture transformed, and I, too, sat a little more upright.

"I have to get that. My apologies."

Shocking me, he disappeared, darting into the French doors.

I closed my eyes, fighting to listen. Was it a wife? Girlfriend? Child?

"Yes?" he answered.

Shamelessly, I eavesdropped.

"Any priors?"

Hmm. I wondered if he was a cop. He didn't seem like a cop. He seemed more professional.

Once his words became more garbled, I turned my head toward the sky. What seemed like a million stars decorated the night. Each one represented an angel...the stars and redbirds...Angels among us. That's what Mimi and Pops always said—the best grandparents ever.

As I lay there, I picked Mimi out of the millions of stars like I always did. Whatever night, whatever day, she was always the biggest and the brightest. Tonight, she was super bright for some reason.

Mr. Make Me Come Just Right was still talking as I closed my eyes.

When I opened my eyes, the sun blared down, and I gasped for a breath. A down comforter snuggled around me, and I sprang upright trying to remember the night before. The balcony was chilly without the comforter. And mainly because I was naked!

Jenner. Jenner! "Jenner?" I said out loud, trying to recall what had happened after the phone call. I couldn't remember anything.

No answer. On my feet, my knees wobbled for a minute before I gained solid footing. My head silently cussed me for the amount of alcohol I'd consumed the night before. Another reason to avoid alcohol.

Through the French doors, Jenner was still nowhere to be seen. My purse was where I'd left it, and after a quick trip to the bathroom to pee, I grabbed my phone. Sixteen texts and three missed calls from Henley. My battery was about dead.

It didn't take me long to go from one end of the suite to the other and to determine I'd been ditched. The place was empty. Vacated.

I spotted a folded piece of paper next to the coffee maker and darted to it so fast, I pulled my hamstring. An *L* was written on the front.

"I'm sorry I had to leave. I hope your night under the stars was all you had hoped. Take care, J."

"Take care?" I questioned out loud. "That's code for farewell."

I'd never been a jilted lover. Admittedly, his goodbye stung a bit. Not that we would be a happily ever after, but last night was the first time in a long time I'd allowed myself to feel. To want. And now I wanted more. I certainly wanted to shed the "V" card. Knowing how attentive Jenner was and knowing how skilled he seemed, I had really wanted to lose it specifically to him.

My phone rang, and I rushed limping to the counter with crossed fingers that it was Jenner. It wasn't. It was Henley.

"Hey," I answered.

"Are you ok? You never called. You haven't texted. I'm at the farmers market."

Shit!

"Yes. I'm fine. I forgot."

"Is that because you got some boo-tay last night?"

"Hardly." I slid my pants on and shoved my feet into my shoes at the same time embarrassed at not closing the deal.

"Where are you?"

"The Waldorf. Don't ask," I said with a threat looming. I shoved my bra into my purse, buttoned my blouse and untied the stupid sides I'd tied in a pathetic, feeble attempt to look sexy last night. "Let me get outta here. I'll call you once I get close."

Tossing my phone in my purse, I slung it over my shoulder and took one last glance around the plush suite that I hadn't really gotten a chance to enjoy. *We* hadn't gotten to enjoy. Then I spotted a bottle on the counter near the sink. Next to the bottle of water was a small packet of ibuprofen, a packet of acetaminophen and another small note.

Monica, My guess is your head hurts. Pick A or B or both. Hopefully, you're not overthinking. No regrets. I believe, what little I know of you, you will be frustrated that you fell asleep (possibly passed out). But let me reassure you, the pleasure was all mine. Thank you. Richard

Wow, he read me well. Popping both sets of pills in my mouth, I downed them with a douse of water, tossed the notes in my purse and left the suite behind.

A line had formed at our normal spot at the Farmer's Market—mostly the usual people, but I saw a few new faces. Henley was waiting for me. Hank had parked Pop's dually into the spot. The entire bed of the truck was loaded with all the fruits and veggies. I loved that Hank and his sons helped with the harvest.

"Running late, darlin?" Hank asked.

I shot him a smile. "Just a smidgin'."

Hank had been my grandfather's best friend for most of his life. He was Pop's best man when he married my Mimi. Heck, on occasion, Hank's sons brought the truck when he couldn't.

As I set a basket of strawberries on the table, he touched my arm.

"You ok, little miss?"

I nodded. "Yes. Just late. I'm sorry."

"You look tired."

Hank's cowboy boots were tired. I grinned. "Late night celebrating, Hank. Maybe a little too much." I winked at him. "Besides, when you tell a girl she looks tired, that's code for she looks like shit."

"Ah, little miss, never never." He darted around me and started helping Henley load the tables with the crop. Before we knew it, we were up and selling for Pops.

All of our regulars came by the tent, and every single one asked about Pops. Most everyone knew about his condition and expressed condolences for the sad situation. Those same people loved chatting with Hank.

The sun warmed the late summer morning as we cleaned up the tables. Henley nudged me in the side. The ache in my head had subsided thanks to the pills. I smiled as I thought about Jenner's considerate gesture. He didn't have to write the notes, nor did he have to track down pocket packs of medicine, but he had.

"There's the guy you wouldn't tell me about."

I froze with a wide-eyed stare, refusing to turn around. "The guy from the club?" I whispered.

She nodded slowly, following him with her eyes.

"Does he see us? Me?" I casually walked to the front of the truck to stay hidden.

What were the freaking odds of running into the man that had his fingers inside me last night? Dear God. The pounding in my chest stole my breath.

"Hey, Lucy, I got the truck loaded with the bushel baskets and…"

"SHH!" I shushed Hank, paralyzed in fear.

Seriously, the likelihood of seeing this man, less than 24 hours later, in New York freaking City? I massaged my temples trying to think.

"What's the matter, little miss?"

"Guy trouble, Hank," Henley answered.

"Is he with anyone?" I asked.

She nodded. "Yes. A woman."

"He's married. I knew it."

"Well, unless he's married to a sixty year old woman, I don't think that's his wife."

For some odd reason, relief settled through me. The guy hadn't asked to see me again. He hadn't texted or called. It was what it was—a very lame one nighter because he just had to answer that damn phone and I couldn't stay awake.

"Well, little miss. If I don't say so myself, I'd have to say you've takin' a likin' to the guy or you wouldn't care if he sees you."

My eyes narrowed in the evilest of glares in Hank's direction until I conceded that he was right.

"I did like him," I said, my eyes darting between both Hank and Henley.

Henley excitedly rose up on her tiptoes. "I have an idea. Where is your phone?"

I pulled it out of my back pocket. "Why?"

"Do you have his number?"

"Yes," I said, but then remembered that the man didn't text.

"Text him. Some sort of 'hey' or 'thank you' or 'want to do it again' something or other."

I bit down on my lip, hoping Hank didn't catch on.

"Why would I do that?"

"Because we can see his reaction. If he smiles, he's happy to hear from you. If he doesn't, fine. Leave it alone."

It was the 'if he doesn't part' that threatened to hurt. Hurt? I'd known him for 12 whole hours, for God's sake. I sounded like a pathetic, desperate girl. But yet, I stared at the phone in my hand.

"Whatcha got to lose?" Hank asked.

I unlocked my phone and typed, as his words came back to me, 'I don't text.'

Hey Richard. I was thinking…that room might have late check-out. Monica

Oh, I felt sick. This was so not me. I glanced up at Henley and Hank, and then hit send.

"What'd you say?" Henley asked.

I shrugged. "Just asked if he wanted to meet up later," I lied for Hank's benefit. Or mine. Whatever.

The three of us literally bent over the hood of the truck to see Jenner through the cab window. We all three watched as he slid his hand in his pocket, the same hand that got me off last night. I hoped he stayed facing this way so I could see his expression. Aviators covered his eyes but I waited to see if he smiled.

Score! Not a full-blown smile but a grin. Slight grin.

Henley squealed. My phone vibrated and I suddenly had two sets of eyes on me.

Opening the screen, a blue dot sat next to his number. I hadn't even

25

entered his name into my contacts. I pushed the text to open it.

This isn't Richard.

I grinned too.
"What did he say?"
I texted back ignoring my audience.

Hey, Mr. Answer the Phone During Foreplay. Do-over?

When I hit send and glanced up, both Hank and Henley looked immediately toward Jenner, who stood behind the lady he was with while she bought a pumpkin. A bigger grin! My phone vibrated.

I wouldn't have answered that call had I not been obligated to do so. Are you sober?

I giggled.

Sober-ish

I was stone cold sober. That text led to another smile.

Lucy sober. Interesting. Penthouse Suite 1402 in two hours?

My fists closed in a silent celebratory moment.
"Yes!" Henley hissed. "When are you seeing him?"
Hanks eyes flashed back and forth between Henley and mine, confused.
"Today. I need to go," I told them, already thinking about what I'd wear.
"You two arranged a date without saying a word to each other?" Hank asked baffled.
Henley and I both laughed, patting Hank's shoulder. "That's how we do it now a days, Hank."

He shook his head. "I might have to meet this guy, Little Miss. I'm not sure Pops would approve. Nor would I."

There was no way to explain to Hank that this was strictly a booty call. Though the explanation of a hook up would be comical, I simply couldn't bring myself to do it. Once we loaded up the truck, I bee-lined it for the apartment and a quick shower.

CHAPTER 2

DISMISSED

Jenner

Once I got Mom settled back at her place, I put the produce she bought away. I had an hour to get to the hotel. Everything in my brain shouted at me to not go, to leave Lucy hanging. To be the bad guy. But there was something adorable about this girl. Overhearing her conversation with her friend had certainly made my dick twitch—knowing she'd not been with anyone for a while. We didn't go to that club often. But Jeff had wanted to find a girl for his birthday. The guys knew that I never took anyone home, so there would be questions later.

This morning as I watched her sleep before I left, I couldn't put my finger on what it was about her. The dress shirt tied in a knot did a number on me. Her beauty was enough to get the attention of anyone in the club, but then she went and did that. Her strawberry blond hair pillowed out around the balcony lounger. The twelve little freckles dotting her nose were so damn irresistible.

Honestly, I hadn't been fucked in a while either. When she had bellowed out that ridiculous request for me to have sex with her, I was stunned, profoundly shocked by the question. Nothing shocked me anymore. But she did. Everything about her. Her innocence. Her courage. Her obliviousness to her own beauty.

I was hard again just thinking about how wet she got for me. The feeling of her insides pulsing around my fingers as I got her off—drove me mad. There was nothing I wanted more than to do that again for her. Knowing she hadn't had that for a while, knowing I could give it to her, watching the pleasure on her face, I couldn't wait to see her.

The lobby was full. I was thankful I'd called about late checkout. We had until 3 PM. I already knew that wouldn't be enough time. I considered getting the room again but didn't want to give her unnecessary hope. I grabbed another key at the front desk.

"Sir. A lady just requested a key but she wasn't listed on the room. I apologize. She's in the hotel bar."

I smiled at him. She had come...

LUCY

The first vodka water went down with ease and the second was just as quick, calming the nerves I'd walked in with. I still didn't know Jenner's last name, so getting a key to his room was impossible. I had rushed home after our conversation, and quicker than I thought possible, I showered and shaved (for the second consecutive day in a while) then found the only other pair of sexy panties I owned. Two was it. I'd never been much of a Victoria's Secret girl. Panties from Target worked just fine.

"Miss, the key to your room," the concierge said sliding the card toward my drink.

Before I could ask anything, he disappeared. I finished my drink like it was a shot and then hopped off the barstool. I second-guessed myself for wearing a dress. Suddenly, it seemed forward. Then again, there were no false pretenses about what this was or why we were meeting. Besides, it would give easy access.

Another couple rode with me in the elevator but got off three floors before the top, leaving me to sweat it out alone.

"Hey, Jenner. Hel-lo, Jenner. Hi!" I changed my voice, practicing from casual to chipper, unsure which would be best.

When the doors opened, there he was dressed in jeans and a long-sleeved polo shirt.

"Whoa. Hey. Umm. Hel-lo! Hi." Wow, I sounded absolutely

ridiculous as I rattled off every greeting I had practiced.

"Hola," he said, his brows shooting up.

"Si!" I laughed. "I don't know much Spanish. Queso. I know queso."

That grin I had sought from him earlier appeared again.

"How are you?" he asked. "Headache gone?

"Yes. Thanks to you."

The room seemed smaller than it did last night. And Jenner seemed bigger. When he tipped his head to the side it was as if he was trying to read me.

"Hmm. You seem to be thinking," I said.

"I'm always thinking."

"About?"

"The phone call last night was not an indicator of my desire. It was a professional obligation."

Tucking my feet beneath me, I sat on the sofa. He leaned against the counter with his ankles crossed.

"What do you do?" I asked.

His heavy gaze never left mine nor did he speak a word.

"OK. You'd prefer I not ask questions?"

"Not that question."

"That's fair. You speak…professionally."

"Probably just me utilizing my Word Wealth class from high school. Mrs. Mowder was a stickler for us applying the words in real life."

I nodded with a grin. "I'm sorry for falling asleep on you."

"Don't be. I'm actually very boring."

A chuckle vibrated across my tummy. "You make me laugh."

"Good. You make me laugh too. Tell me what you want, Lucy. The last thing I want to do is mislead you."

His question caused me to sit up a little straighter. "Well, a replay of last night for starters without the phone call and without the falling asleep part."

A smirk pulled at the side of his mouth. "That's doable. I'm doable." He winked. "I'm not sure how much I have to offer past that."

"You're married?"

"No. And, I'm not gay either."

Unknowingly, I bit down on my lip. "I'm glad. I won't lie, I like you. What little I know of you. But if we can't be, we can't be. I'm not gonna go all *Fatal Attraction* on you."

With a chuckle of laughter, he raked his hands through his hair. I wanted my hands in his hair.

"You going *Fatal Attraction* isn't my concern. I'll be truthful as well. I like you too. I just know what I'm capable of and what I'm not. Taking that into consideration, I don't want you feeling rejected. If I state the facts up front..."

Already feeling rejection as he said those words. I nodded. "Rejection is simply redirection, Jenner. Sometimes it hurts, but I'll do my best to redirect myself." Hopefully my subtle smile was enough reassurance for him.

"OK, then stand up," he said. His tone dropped an entire octave and vibrated something in my pelvis.

I stood, my breath hitching in my throat as his eyes devoured me inch by inch. Still leaning against the counter, he beckoned me with his finger. I inched closer.

His finger was soft, not callused, as it traced over my shoulder, beneath the spaghetti strap, freeing the material from my shoulder. The strap drooped down my arm. The dress was now being held up by one strap. But that didn't last long as he repeated the motion on the other side, sending the dress to pool at my feet.

His tongue ran the length of his bottom lip.

"You are very beautiful."

Several men had said those words to me, but for some reason Jenner saying them meant something more. His words...his approval... mattered.

"Thank you," I whispered.

His fingertips traced over the mounds of my breasts, sparking them to life. I leaned into him, grazing my fingers over his zipper, somewhat nervous to touch him.

"You know," he said, clearing his throat. "There was something about watching you come that I thoroughly enjoyed."

The simply spoken statement shot a quake of desire rippling through my body. Electricity fired up through my abdomen, igniting my nipples, pebbling them up. And, an entire other line fueled the need between my legs. A surge of dampness pooled in my panties.

A masculine smell wafted through the air stimulating me even more. My eyes instinctively closed as the backs of his fingers slid beneath the lace. My nipple glided between two of his fingers, and he lightly squeezed them together.

"Jenner," I whispered, and it sounded more like a rush of air.

Like a pro, his other hand reached around back, unfastening my bra. The release was pleasurable as heaviness fell into my breasts. He bent down, his knees cracking, and traced his tongue around my nipple. He gently sucked it into his mouth, my legs weakened and nearly gave way.

He stopped, glancing up at me. His eyes were dark, intimidating, lust filled and his lids stood at half-mast.

"Come on," he said, taking hold of my hand and leading me to the bedroom. We never got this far last night.

When he stopped next to the bed, it was me that dropped to my knees. I wanted to please him too. The minute I tried to unfasten his pants, he stopped me.

"Lucy. You don't know me well enough to do that. As much as I'd like for you to."

This man didn't mince words. His casual directness seemed harsh.

"O. K." I said ok as if it were two separate words. My mood squashed just a bit.

He lifted my chin. "Lucy. Don't. Don't take that personally, ok?"

For not knowing me very well, he certainly knew me well.

"Have you been with a lot of people without protection?" I asked surprised standing back up.

He shook his head. "No. None. Ever. This…" His Adams apple jutted out and back in. "This is odd for me as well."

"I'm not sure I understand."

"Well, I'm not sure what I'm saying," he chuckled but with no laughter in his eyes. "You trust so easily. Had I been someone else, anyone else, last night may have ended entirely different."

Suddenly, I felt like he was my father chastising me. Things were getting weird. I released a long, slow, exasperated exhale. "I understand that." I gave a resigned sigh, sitting back on the bed.

"Yes, but you have no idea where I've been."

"You just said, you'd been with no one!"

"Exactly my point," he said emotionless. "What makes me believable? Guys will say anything to get in your pants."

"What guy says no to getting a blow job?"

He tilted his head to the side, that slow, half-smile making an appearance. "You want me to wear a condom, yes?"

"Yes."

"Jesus Christ, I sound like an old man. You can catch something from giving a blow job too."

"I'm aware of that." I was totally aware of that.

"OK, tell me what you prefer then, and I'm just going to shut up now."

"Jenner, do you even want to do this? Pity sex isn't really my thing. And though I like you, I don't really want to guilt you into doing something you'd prefer not to."

Suddenly, he grabbed hold of my wrist, pushing my hand against his rock hard, bulging crotch.

"Sometimes, I'm not very good attaching emotion to words. I get paid to keep emotions out of most equations."

"Well," I laughed a little. "I prefer you not use words like equation or attaching emotion and just enjoy the moment maybe."

"Forgive me. Tell me what you want, pretty girl. What do you prefer?" he grinned.

God, there was something sexy about his grin; the moment I bit down on my bottom lip, his thumb pulled it free. I wasn't sure if I wanted to walk out the penthouse door or finish what we started.

"What do I prefer? Hmmm. I'd prefer you text me when this is over. Even if you don't want to." I smiled. "It'll make me feel better about myself. So, send me something just to make me smile. Umm. I'd prefer that you never speak of this to anyone. I know all the girls that do this sort of thing say they aren't that sort of girl." I tossed up air quotes. "But I really don't do this sort of thing." His eyes bore into me. "I'd prefer you have no regrets. I promise I won't either. I'd also prefer you tell me what to do and when to do it because honestly, I'm very intimidated by this and, I just think that I need some guidance and…"

His fingertips pressed over my lips shushing me. There was something about his touch that electrified every inch of my body. His fingertips brought me to life.

"Lucy. You are very persuasive. I'd prefer that you go ahead and get on your knees for a bit then," he whispered, gently pushing my shoulders down. My eyes widened as he unbuttoned his jeans allowing them to fall.

Immediately, I knelt gazing up at him, watching as he inched his boxer briefs down exposing himself to me. Instinctively, my mouth fell open like a baby bird waiting for its treat. I wasn't sure what to do but I'd seen it done in movies. It couldn't be that complicated.

With his thumb, Jenner directed it toward my mouth and I took it. Proudly, I took all of it, my gag reflex engaged making my eyes water. As if he knew, he pulled back just a bit. But when his fingertips traced along my jaw line that comforted me. There was something beyond lust in his eyes. With one hand, I reached around and held his butt cheek, setting a rhythm. The next time I peeked up at him, his neck was angled back—his breathing more sporadic. I smiled, which was actually quite hard. This really wasn't just about me, I decided in that moment.

Keeping pace, my own body responded as I thought about what I was doing to him and about what he had done to me last night with only a couple of fingers. My pace quickened as thoughts consumed me.

"Stop, Lucy," he said firmly, pulling out of my mouth. His thumb traced over my bottom lip. "I'd *prefer* not to come yet." He winked, pulling me to my feet. The tenderness in his fingers as he touched my nipples sent a ripple of pleasure through me.

"However, you coming is completely preferable."

I smiled as his fingertips pushed my panties to the side and then worked their way through my wetness.

A low moan scraped up my throat as he buried a finger inside of me. Immediately, his thumb found the most sensitive part of my body, and he began to set a pace of his own.

I didn't want to be standing. I wanted to lie down and enjoy every second of this… Every. Single. Second. The fuse was lit. Burning. Detonation loomed. His teeth bit down on my ear lobe.

"You're so fucking sexy," he growled near my ear. "Especially when you're about to come."

My knees nearly buckled as the pleasurable feeling in my abdomen grew. Suddenly, his finger was gone. My eyes shot open.

"I'd *prefer* you not stop," I said, panting.

There was that grin. "Look, little miss…" he said softly. Hearing him say that familiar name brought a grin to my flushed face. Even though it typically came from Hank or Pops, the sentiment wasn't lost on me. "You said you'd prefer that I tell you what to do and when to do it." He slid my panties over my hips until they fell to the ground. "I'll let you know when to come."

"No." I shook my head. "That is not at all what I meant."

A soft chuckle came from his chest. "Lie down."

I did as he said but was lost in a fog of lust. I'd do anything he asked.

He lifted his jeans off the floor and retrieved a condom from the pocket. I watched him as I lay there full of need, full of want, full of desire. All I wanted was to be full of him.

The look on his face matched what I felt on mine. His eyes flashed back and forth between my face and my body. He brushed a kiss over my hipbone, then the tip of my nose as he positioned himself over me. The weight of him rested between my legs, and I spread my thighs a little more to allow him full access.

My heart found a steady rhythm when I released my held breath. I knew this was probably going to hurt, but dear Lord did I want him to take me. When he arched his hips—BINGO…his head began to enter me. Slowly. Deliberately. Jenner slid smoothly, perfectly, effortlessly and painfully inside of me. By the look on his face it seemed painful for him too.

"My God…" I whimpered, bracing myself for the full invasion.

I fought looking into his eyes—secretly, I knew I'd fall for even the smallest amount of confirmation. Our chemistry, to me, was undeniable. Yet, for whatever reason he couldn't or wouldn't give more.

"You ok?" he spoke softly, and instantly my eyes were drawn to his. I nodded.

"Welcome back," he whispered, brushing a kiss over my forehead; he never kissed my lips.

"Why would one go without this?" I groaned as he pulled out and then slid as agonizingly slow back in. I wondered what he might have thought of a 24-year-old virgin as the stretched skin burned.

He grinned. "Poor decision on your part. Though had you not gone without, this may have never happened."

My hips arched up once again to meet his gentle thrust.

"Yep, we were meant to be." After the words seeped out, regret consumed me. But his eyes held mine as if he agreed with the admission. As if...

His eyes closed, shutting me off from the emotion mirrored there. I closed mine too. If this was the first and only time with Jenner—fate was playing a cruel joke.

The weight of his body was gone, and my lids flew open. While still inside of me, he'd risen to his knees. This angle was painful in the beginning. My half-mast eyes watched as he slid his thumb into my wetness, and then began to massage my clit once again. The feeling from before immediately revived to life. Damn, the pleasure. The building of what was one of the most pleasurably satisfying feelings in the world. A feeling that I never wanted to live without again. Not even for a day. I wanted Jenner to provide that feeling. Over the past couple of years, I had never given anyone the opportunity, nor did I trust anyone enough to cave to the feeling. But now, I didn't want to let it go. It was in that moment between knowing I was going to come and feeling him thrust inside that I decided I would do whatever it took to change his mind. I had to change his mind to see me again.

"Jenner..." I cried out just as I exploded. Last night it had been around his finger, tonight it was around his dick. Multiple waves of pleasure spilled across my abdomen.

"Jesus, Lucy. I can feel you coming around me."

As the orgasm waned, my hips bucked up wanting to help him find his. The pleasure of pleasing him was satiating in and of itself.

"You trying to make me come?"

I bit down on my lip as my hips continued.

"Yes, beautiful girl. I'm gonna come."

Immediately, I stopped moving my hips…I mean like a complete standstill, and his lustful look of pleasure turned to a look of shock. His wide-eyed stare found only a shitty grin when he looked down at me.

"Doesn't feel so good when you just stop, huh?" I teased, desire coloring my tone.

The right side of his mouth pulled up just a bit into a slight smile.

"You want to play games?" he asked trying to slide into me, but I squeezed my thighs together preventing full entry. The torn skin around my opening burned.

Suddenly, he pulled completely out, flipped me over to my belly, smacked my ass and buried himself in me from behind.

"Jenner!" I shouted as he robbed me of breath. There was no possible way he could have known how much that would have hurt someone who'd never had sex. John Mellencamp's Hurt so Good screamed in my head.

Jenner's voice was right next to my ear. "Yes, Lucy?" he asked in a rough whisper, once again finding a very satisfying pace.

I simply shook my head, trying to gather my thoughts. This man was perfect. I had no words.

"I'm going to come, Lucy. I'm going to use this beautiful, fucking body to do it. Do you understand?"

I nodded. Barely. But it was a nod, nonetheless. This wasn't just losing my virginity. More like a homerun into womanhood. A blessing and a curse.

"Tell me you want that, Lucy."

His thrusts, more powerful than before, were coming quicker. I welcomed every inch of him but knew soreness would be evident tomorrow. I worried about blood tonight. My opening burned where the tender, mistreated skin had torn.

"I don't hear you telling me…"

I smiled into the mattress. All I could think was: that's because you're drilling me!

"Yes," I finally said not even sure what I was saying yes to.

"Yes, what?"

Excellent question.

"I don't know," I admitted. I could barely remember my name.

He chuckled, slowing his pace.

"Lucy, my sweet."

I smiled at his condescending tone.

"Tell me that you want me to come."

"Oh, God, yes. Please. Please."

The places he touched inside of me…not just physically but emotionally…mentally. He kept me on my toes—the same toes that curled in anticipation of his thrusts.

Our bodies made the sweetest sounds as they slapped together.

"Christ, Lucy," he gritted as his hands tightened on my hips before he buried himself deep inside of me. I yelped. Literally yelped like a wounded dog. My body was stretched beyond capacity as I felt him pulse inside of me. Soft, baritone groans sang out into the room as his body collapsed onto mine. Feeling the weight of his body on me was heavy but heavenly.

The sliver of sunlight seeping through the curtain was a sign that our time was running out. Our life-line waning. For a second, I felt like Julia Roberts in *Pretty Woman*. Her perfect life existed inside that hotel room with Richard Gere. The outside world wasn't in the cards for us. Reality sometimes sucked.

Following a long stretch of silence, a few soft kisses, and getting dressed, we met at the door. My body and mind spent, the sadness held tight to me.

"Well," he started.

"Jenner," I giggled, but it was a nervous giggle. "I promise I won't make this more difficult than what it should be. Thank you. Thank you for being that guy."

"The pleasure was mine."

"I'm serious. So many things I did shouted 'psycho'. Asking if you were gay. The Welcome to the Jungle comment. Asking you to have sex with me."

"That last one was my favorite." His eyes twinkled. "I never thought you were a psycho. Adorable. Drunk. Sexy. But not psycho."

I leaned up on my toes and softly pecked his lips. "Thank you."

When I turned to leave, he wrapped his fingers around the back of my neck and yanked me back. There's that moment before a kiss happens where the anticipation hangs between you. His glance moved from my eyes to my lips, and then suddenly, his mouth covered mine in a kiss. Our first kiss really. A soft, memorable kiss. And just when I thought he was done, his tongue slipped into my mouth searching for mine. I wondered if he knew this was only making it harder to say goodbye. I wished it were the beginning, not the end.

No girl wanted to hear 'thanks for the fuck, now goodbye.' But damn, a goodbye like this should end up with at the very least an 'I'll call you later.' Yet when the kiss drew to an end, our words fell short. Silence once again.

"Goodbye, Richard."

"So long, Monica."

When I turned away, he wore that shitty little grin that I'd fallen in love with in the matter of 24 hours.

I waited, breath held, to see if he stopped the elevator. Stopped me from leaving. But, the doors closed and the elevator chimed with each floor that passed. My phone buzzed, and I pulled it from my purse.

I hadn't put Jenner's name in my phone, but I recognized the number immediately. I couldn't open it fast enough. I wondered if this was the text I asked for.

Remember out in the middle of the ocean when Wilson got away from Tom Hanks in Castaway and Tom cried out as the ball floated farther and farther away?

I smiled and typed back.

Yes…

Yep. Me too.

I stared at the words on the screen unsure how to take them.

Am I the volleyball in this scenario?

The elevator dinged, and I stepped out, still staring at my phone. I'm sure everyone in the lobby saw that I had that freshly fucked look about me, but I couldn't have cared less. Finally, my phone vibrated.

Yes ma'am.

I squealed. Literally squealed. Yelping and squealing all within the same hour. What was happening to me? I inhaled, trying to gather my thoughts, then finally sent back:

Tom was never the same without Wilson. Maybe you shouldn't let the volleyball get away...

Four hours later, I still clutched my phone as I got my clothes out for the workday tomorrow, still waiting for a response. Nothing came.

CHAPTER 3

PRO SE

Lucy

My nerves sent my stomach into my throat as I stepped foot in the courtroom. This was my third day of work and my fourth day of not hearing from Jenner. Every night I'd laid in bed thinking about our time together. How good being with him felt. And, it wasn't just the sex. Our conversations…our laughter…our teasing—all of it.

Even though the past four days my body had spent healing from being torn apart by Jenner, my body needed him or maybe it just craved sex in general. But I didn't think so. I couldn't imagine sex with anyone but him. But, I couldn't think about that right now. Right now, I had to focus. Today was my debut—my solo flight. I'd been in a courtroom a hundred times as an intern but this time, I was officially acting as prosecutor. The navigator of the case. Inhaling the deepest of breaths, I sat at the State's table and organized the folders and papers in the way that I would need them. Child in need of care wasn't where any attorney really wanted to work, but I did. I'd become an attorney for exactly this. Working for the New York County DA was a great start.

The file was small for the temporary custody hearing and was literally thrown at me after lunch. I'd done one of my internships in child in need of care court in a different county, therefore I felt pretty confident. The guardian ad litem came in and sat next to me.

"Hey, Deb."

"Hey. How's it going, Lucy?'

"Flying solo on day three. I'm a bit nervous."

"First appearance in front of Judge Weber?"

I nodded. "Yes, ma'am."

"You ever met him?"

"Nope. This is my first appearance."

"Well, get ready to have your breath taken away. He sexy as fuck but don't hold your breath. He doesn't consort or fraternize with us common folk. His father is a supreme. He's better than us and lets you know it."

"A supreme? Like state supreme?"

"All rise."

The moment the words were spoken, my heart began to beat out of my chest, but it wasn't until Jenner strolled through the chamber door in a pressed black robe that I felt faint. Literally faint; my head swam.

No. No. No. No. This wasn't happening. Jenner Weber? Judge Jenner Weber? The Honorable Jenner Weber? Dear God. Indiana Jones—virginity nabber.

"Thank you. You may be seated," he announced and I sat or collapsed.

He hadn't seen me yet. I watched waiting for his eyes to land on me. My heart beat like the rattle of a snake. The folder he reviewed had to be the case we were here for.

"The court calls the case 17JC2091. May I have the appearances please?"

There it was. His eyes lifted to meet mine. A brief moment of hesitation. The last time his eyes were on me, his dick was inside of me. Ok...not quite, but close.

I stood, my knees trembling. "May it please the court, Lucy Edwards appearing for the State." I had no idea how those words came out.

His serious eyes shifted from me to the guardian ad litem with almost no appearance of recognition. It required effort to listen to her words. Then it was my turn again.

Jenner roughly cleared his throat. "Ms. Edwards, State's position?"

Wobbly knees and all, I got to my feet again. "Yes, Your Honor. Um. Based off the state's petition, we are requesting the newborn respondent be placed in the custody of the Department of Children and Families. Yesterday, the newborn tested positive for opiates and heroin, after delivery. The baby remains in the neonatal unit suffering from withdrawals. The mother, Heather Cook, admitted to using prior to going to the hospital to give birth. Clearly, Your Honor, the health, safety and welfare of this child are at risk. The State is requesting the child remain at the hospital in the temporary custody of the agency. Thank you."

"Ms. Scheels?"

"Thank you, Judge. I concur with the state and would ask for a no-contact order with parents unless DCF can secure supervised visits at the hospital."

Damn it. I should have thought of that. Jenner wrote something down and then his eyes moved to the parent's attorney.

"Mr. Gibson?"

"Your Honor. Parents are not objecting to custody. However, they are opposed to supervised visits. They have not shown any indication of fleeing with the baby or any indication of putting the child at risk."

I shot up out of my chair. "We object, Your Honor. They haven't put the baby at risk? The mother used heroin prior to birth, drugging herself and her baby with a highly addictive drug. The baby is in the neonatal intensive care unit, Judge. The State would be opposed. If the parents can provide a negative urinalysis prior to the visit, then we would not be opposed."

Jenner's eyes bore into me, then quickly flitted back to the bench at the papers before him. As much as I should have been thinking about that baby, the only thing on my mind was the shock in my heart and the heat between my legs. So many things flashed through my mind. He knew my name. I knew his.

"Based on probable cause, the court is ruling in favor of the State. The child will immediately go into police-protective custody until DCF can get workers assigned. I'm ordering UA's on the parents to begin prior to any supervised visit. This matter will be set for pre-trial on the next docket September 17. All parties are ordered to reappear. Is there anything further to come before the court at this time?"

"No, Your Honor," I said softly, and all other parties stayed silent.

"Hearing nothing further, this matter is in recess," Jenner gruffly spat out and stormed from the courtroom, file in hand.

"Wow, he seems even testier than normal," Deb whispered.

Offering a nervous smile, I stacked my papers, not caring anymore about their organization. I'd organize and take notes of what happened when I returned to my office. When my brain could work again. I silently prayed my legs would get me there.

"Hey, Lucy. It wasn't you. You did nothing wrong," Deb said, sliding her file in her briefcase.

Oh my God. If she only knew. If she only knew? If anyone knew! My breakfast from earlier churned in my stomach, threatening to come right back up.

"Lucy? You ok?"

"Yep. Just taking it all in. My first official court appearance."

Free from the courtroom and finally in the hall, the air cooled my face as I walked. My erratic breaths were starting to settle, but my brain synapses couldn't keep up with the mile-a-minute activity snapping off. The second I got to my desk, I found my cell phone to see if there was something…anything… from Jenner. There wasn't. Weber? So, he was related to Supreme Court Justice Weber… like United States Supreme Court Judge… Fuck me.

That night at home, I kept my phone by my side. Hoping. Waiting. Dreading. I started to text him fifteen times. I typed out long texts, shorts texts and finally, I settled for simple.

Jenner?

CHAPTER 4

ETHICAL CODE

Jenner

When my phone vibrated, I knew immediately it was Lucy. I literally never texted. Rarely. Only with the guys. Texts can and will be used against you in a court of law. I opened the text right away. I wanted to know what she had to say. Fuck, I had wanted to text her all day. Email. Call. But I couldn't. I wouldn't.

As I poured myself some bourbon, my mind reeled with the reality of what had happened. Nearly nine million people in the county and I just happen to fuck the new assistant DA assigned to my courtroom? I relaxed back in my recliner with my dick hard as a rock as I thought about her wearing that black little pencil skirt and pressed blue blouse. Her body would fit anything perfectly. Including me.

I downed the amber liquid quicker than usual; that nice Kentucky bourbon hugged my throat. How did I not see her being a lawyer? Never once did attorney cross my mind. She was such a funny, free spirit in bed. Out of bed too. Yet, as I lay there, I realized how she challenged me. Her texts about Castaway and Wilson and not letting the volleyball go. Her wit. Here was someone I could really engage with on more than a physical level. Fuck!

I glanced at her text once again, thinking about her hands…her fingers typing it out. I thought about her hands as they gripped my cock. Her hands as they cupped my balls. Her hands clawing at the sheets four nights ago as I took her from behind. She was so damn tight. If I engaged tonight, knowing what I knew at this point, my ass would be on the line even more than before. Listening to her verbalize the State's claims today in her petition and reason for removal had been difficult. I actually had to fight hard to pay attention to her words. I knew she had been as flustered as I. Composure had to be maintained. So I did. I certainly couldn't recuse myself from my cases—I somehow had to get her off the CINC rotation in the DA's office. Though, the credibility of the cases we worked together until such time would be in question with the ethics board if someone found out.

I opened my law book and read: *Professional Code of Ethics*: Canon 3E/Rule 2.11(A) –Disqualification may be required if, under the general "catchall" standard, a judge's impartiality might reasonably be questioned if –Presiding over cases involving an attorney with whom the judge had a romantic relationship.

My father would turn over on his supreme bench if he knew what was happening. He had been my age when he reached district court status and quickly moved up to appeals and circuit court. The bar was set when the last president appointed him to the Supreme Court. And it was because of my father that I was forced to become a judge, and even more because of him that I hadn't had a serious relationship my entire life. Douglas James Henry Weber was a shit father and an even shittier husband. I wanted no part of either marriage or fatherhood because of him.

My phone vibrated again. It would be easier if I just hit delete without reading the text, but every part of who I was wanted to know what she had to say. After this weekend and my time with her, I thirsted for her words.

Please say something…

Irritated, I tossed my phone on the nightstand, rolled over and went to bed. Staying strong was my only option if I was going to maintain an ounce of credibility in my profession.

CHAPTER 5

JUDICIAL WARNING

Lucy

Two long, torturous days had passed since I'd seen Jenner in court. I stood in the hallway of Division 14 mustering up the courage to go in. In my hands, was a motion to remove a nine-year-old girl from her home. The judge's signature was a requirement or I wouldn't be standing in the hallway. His hallway.

I'd worn my high-waist black slacks today with a white, fitted dress shirt. Great thought went into every single outfit I wore to work just in case Jenner and I crossed paths at some time during my day.

Exactly as anticipated, this was the day I'd see him again. Two days after he ignored my texts. Courage brewed beneath the surface of my skin as I inhaled the deepest of breaths with eyes closed.

"You ok, Miss Edwards?"

Startled by his voice, my eyes shot wide. He walked right past me.

"Jenner." His name flooded out in a rush of air. "I'm... I'm sorry," I stuttered. "I...I mean Judge. Your Honor." Shit. Shit Shit. I toddled behind him but nearly creamed into him when he pivoted around.

"Please address me formally here." His tone was terse.

"Of course." I nodded. "Yes, sir."

At that point, I refused to make eye contact.

"I assume you need to see me if you're taking deep breaths in the hallway. Please come in."

Blood invaded my cheeks. Seriously, being caught taking breaths? He strolled through his office, addressed his administrative assistant as did I with a timid smile, then we both walked into his chambers. The walls decorated only with simple, black-framed diplomas, certificates and credentials of why he sat on the opposite side of the bench as I.

"Have a seat."

I sat. I could smell him and I'd never wished for sensory deprivation more. I didn't want to see him, smell him, taste him, hear him or touch him. Zero. Actually, I wanted all of that.

Once he relaxed into his chair, I stared at him. Just stared.

"What did you need, Miss Edwards?"

"Oh." I shot a glance toward the other room where his assistant sat. "I'm sorry. I have an Ex Parte order and a Motion to remove I'd like you to look at, please."

When I handed him the paperwork, our fingers brushed each other's. I couldn't help it; our eyes met then. And there was nothing I could do to pull my stare from his, after the fact. His beautiful, dark eyes flickered from my eyes to my mouth. Without thinking, my tongue slipped out between my lips, moistening them. Following a long thirty seconds, he blinked—desire… memories…possibilities… faded. I took a casual step back as he reviewed the papers. Both of our professional facades back in place, his more than mine.

With his pen, he scribbled notes on the side of the motion, then signed it and the order. If things were based on what I was feeling, I'd ask for another night in the penthouse suite. Even though I couldn't really afford the room but my thoughts and words got stuck in my throat.

After he signed everything, then reviewed it again, he handed it back to me. His desk seemed like an entire country wedged between us.

"Judge, I'm running up to division 6. I'll be back."

His eyes didn't leave mine. "Ok. Thank you, Sara."

When I heard the outer door close, I breathed a little freer. Our audience was gone.

Immediately, he stood. "Ms. Edwards. You can NOT slip and call me Jenner," he said softly, refusing to look at me.

"I know. I know. I'm sorry."

He shook his head. "I don't want apologies. I want compliance."

The terse words stung. All of his words made sense now. The wealth words or whatever it was he called it. The way he spoke. The way he carried himself. No names. No professions. Everything from our night together fell into place. He didn't text—no trail of evidence.

"Is there something else, Ms. Edwards?"

This time his words brought me out of my thoughts.

"Pardon me?"

His jaw was tight. "Do. You. Have. Something. Else?"

I shook my head, tears stinging my eyes. God, he was being a total dick. "No. No, sir."

"Please close the door as you leave." He swiveled around to his computer, dismissing me not only with his words but with his actions as well.

I stood, shocked. No mention of our night. No kindness. Nothing.

Once out of his office, I inhaled and exhaled repeatedly. Breathed in anger, breathed out hurt. Fuck you, Jenner. Fuck you!

CHAPTER 6

DIRECT EVIDENCE

Jenner

"What the hell is wrong with you today?" Alex asked, throwing a towel at me as the sweat trickled down my face and dripped off my nose.

"Nothing's wrong," I lied, panting, trying to beat my personal best on the assault bike. I hated the bike—CrossFit's own torture device. Give me the rower. Ski machine or running any day. But, today, I deserved torture. My quads cried out as I pedaled, but that pain was mild compared to the scream of my lungs. I glanced across the room at the puke bucket. It had been a long time since I'd puked.

How the hell did this happen? My intentional curtness with Lucy had hurt her. I saw it in her eyes. I saw it in her expression. She deserved so much more than me. The day she left me in that hotel room, I prayed I'd never see her again, knowing that after only 24 hours with her… she'd stolen a piece of me. An achievement no other woman had ever accomplished. I should never have sent that damn text about Tom Hanks and Wilson. But, knowing we lived in a sea of people in New York City, who would have thought she'd show up in my damn courtroom.

There was nothing she would find with me except heartbreak. Marriage wasn't in the cards, and kids weren't even in the same deck. Raised by Satan himself, I'd seen firsthand the epitome of a fucked-up marriage, and I wanted no part of it.

"Seriously, Jenner." Alex stopped the arms of the bike.

I glared at him, barely able to catch my breath. "What's your problem, Alex?"

"My problem is—I don't need someone dropping dead in here because they carry in some emotional vendetta and try to take it out on the assault bike. Move on to something else."

He didn't stick around to talk, but I did get off the bike, still eyeballing the bucket.

When I grabbed the pegs of the pegboard and began my assent up the wall, I couldn't breathe. The emotion rearing up inside like a volcano pissed me off. This…exercise… CrossFit…was the only thing I knew to do with it. Halfway up the wall, I was spent and couldn't move the peg another hole. I fell to my back on the mat below staring up at the pegs that no one could reach.

"Slick, Jenner. Real slick."

"Fuck off, Alex."

CHAPTER 7

CONFLICT OF INTEREST

Lucy

Two weeks had passed since I'd seen Jenner. Thoughts of him went through my head at least hourly, sometimes more. A lot times more. Whether it was seeing his name on a document or preparing for a docket or just daydreaming about our time together. I wanted to hate him for the way he treated me…the way he shut me down by basically ignoring me. But, I didn't hate him. He had shot electrical bolts through my body unleashing a need and desire I never understood or realize existed. I'd fought all temptation to text or reach out to him. Pops used to say it's better to have loved and lost than to have never loved at all, but I wasn't sure about that in this case. If I had never felt the way he made my body come alive, then maybe my heart wouldn't incurably yearn for him.

"Lucy. Take this to Judge Weber to get signed. I have to run file a warrant," the juvenile supervisor directed.

I could feel the blood drain from my face.

"I'm swamped. I…"

"You're at the bottom of the totem pole. You can be swamped when you get back."

I nodded. "Ok," I said, taking the papers from her.

"Run it to the clerks office after he signs it."

I rolled my eyes where she couldn't see and slid on my jacket.

The entire walk over to Jenner's office I prepared myself, rehearsing in my head how I hoped this would go down. His unpredictability left me clueless as to what to expect, but I braced myself for the worst.

When I opened the door to his division, his assistant wasn't there. That made me feel minimally better. My pits were sweating, and I was struggling to ward off the oncoming anxiety attack.

"Come in."

Jenner's voice came from his office, and the thought of walking around the corner made me sick. Seeing him would bring every feeling rushing back.

"Hi, Judge. I need to get a paper signed. I'm not sure what it's referencing but..."

"Hand it to me." he interrupted.

It was like he was an entirely different man than the one I had so readily given myself to. That man was funny and attentive. This man wearing the black robe was a complete asshole.

"Who prepared this?"

"I'm not sure. I was asked to run it over since I'm the newbie. Trust me, I didn't volunteer."

His dark eyes darted up to mine, and out of nervous habit my upper teeth came down on my bottom lip.

"I'm not signing this. The motion isn't complete."

"Fine. I'll take it back."

"Watch your tone, Ms. Edwards."

Without the paper in hand, I walked over to the door to make sure his administrative assistant still wasn't there.

"My tone? Is *my* tone really the problem?"

Jenner dropped the papers onto his desk and folded his arms across his chest, then reclined back in his chair. My heart pounded in my throat.

"I'm not in the mood to read between the lines, Ms. Edwards. If you have something to say, why don't you just say it?"

I'm never speechless. Never. My mind raced. I shot back over to the door to be safe. Still no assistant in sight.

"Why do you have to be so mean?" My damn voice cracked, angering me but I was able to hold the tears that threatened to fall at bay.

Jenner's Adam's apple jutted out and back in as he swallowed. Then he closed his eyes with a deep inhale. He was going to blow a gasket, and I couldn't take it.

"Look. This is so hard. I'm sorry. I'm sorry," I said, hoping to prevent the inevitable explosion.

"Don't be sorry. We just…" his words trailed off.

"We just what?"

"Can't. And certainly can't talk about this here. Ever."

"I know," I whispered, and as hard as I fought it, those traitorous tears invaded my eyes. "I had no idea who you were. I just." I paused, fighting the urge to actually cry. "This was such a shock… and I didn't know… and now…this is so hard, Judge."

"Don't call me Judge."

What? I dropped the folder in my hands and covered my eyes. "I am trying. I swear to God. If you weren't who you are… and I don't know how to act around you. One minute you're biting my head off and…" My erratic words trailed off this time. "I want to see you again. But I get it. I really do. That's why you blew me off the other night."

His eyes narrowed. "I didn't blow you off, Lucy. Do you understand that I should recuse myself on every single case that you're assigned? Do you understand that ethically, this isn't acceptable? We both could lose our jobs."

After a deep breath, I retrieved the folder I had dropped and squared my shoulders. "I understand. I won't text you again. No one knows about what happened except us. It's done. Over. No one needs to know it ever happened." My professional tone surprised me. Peeling my eyes away from him, I turned and forced myself to walk toward the door.

"Don't go," he whispered, his voice closer than I expected.

Those two words pierced my heart, stopping me in my tracks. Though I wasn't facing him, I closed my eyes to steady myself. I felt the heat of his body as he placed his hands flush with the wall on either side of me. A silent gasp fled between my lips.

"Miss Edwards." His mouth was in my hair. "The ethics board doesn't care about the tense of our relationship. Past or present. What they care about is that the existence of a relationship could interfere or bias my decisions."

I nodded. "I know. I know this can't happen."

"I'm trying my best to figure out how to keep it from happening."

His words sparked a glimmer of hope, fanning that smoldering desire that I had been trying futilely to smother.

"I would never expect special favors. Special rulings. I'd expect nothing less than for you to be fair and impartial." I gushed, grasping at the lifeline he had tossed me.

"And you think we could be in court together after having my cock inside of you at night? That would be fair and unbiased, yes?"

A ripple of tremors quaked through my body with his dirty talk.

"I don't know," I admitted.

Before I realized it, he'd spun me around and gently pushed me against the wall.

"I'm sorry, Lucy, did you miss ethics class when they taught that in law school?"

Though his face was only inches from mine, I could tell his demeanor had changed. Suddenly agitated, he stared at my face for a few seconds, then spun on his heels, cleared his throat and returned to his desk.

My heart was throwing a serious tantrum in my chest over his Jekyll Hyde shit. Then, of course, I heard the outside door of his office.

"Judge," a woman's voice resonated into the room.

Jenner glanced up at me, his expression unreadable, then said, "Come in, please."

A petite, brunette rounded the corner. "Oh goodness, I didn't mean to interrupt," she said in a squeaky, annoying voice.

"Miss Edwards was just leaving. What can I help you with, Miss McCartney?"

"Please," I said, stepping out of the girl's way. She appeared younger than me. "I'm done here," I added for good measure, picking up the papers I'd brought in, sliding them into the folder. "Thank you, Judge."

My heels clicked loudly with every angry step. Could that man have given more of a mixed message? As my finger punched the elevator button over and over again, I realized I was caught up in an impossible game. One that I could never win. I didn't know how to make him want me. My whole life had been centered around the single purpose of helping children, protecting them. And now, after only one stupid night with this man, I was letting my desire for something I could never have drive me mad—keep me from remaining focused. I needed to get my head on straight. The only game I needed to be in was my career. When I stepped onto the elevator and pushed the button, I decided that staying away from Jenner Weber was in my best interest. As much as I didn't want to, it was my only option.

CHAPTER 8

ADJOURNED

Jenner

Every single day, I read and reread the ethic statute that could end my career. I read it before I took the bench in front of her. I read it at the end of every day, so I wouldn't reach out to her. Over the past 45 days seeing her hadn't gotten easier. I came to work early and left late hoping not to run into Lucy. Seeing her in court was hard enough.

Though I had no interest in staying in the Child in Need of Care juvenile division, Lucy's passion was clear. Each case was an individual fight for her. Each case seemed personal. She was going to save New York County one child at a time. Even more evidence that I wasn't the man for her. Honestly, it was a lost cause. This court did what it could, but the city was overwhelmed. Not enough workers to do the work and half the workers didn't do their jobs well. I wanted to do my time and get out. Lucy was a distraction. Hell, being a judge wasn't what I had wanted to do in the first place. I was here because my asshole of a father hadn't given me a choice.

I peeked out the tinted window of my chamber door. There she sat, prepared and waiting, wearing a silk blouse that hinted at the luscious curves below. I wondered if that was intentional. My dick flinched seeing her. It remembered in vivid detail how good she felt, and regardless of my discouragement, it seemed to have a mind of its own.

I grabbed the green legal folder off my desk and half-heartedly read the file, falling short on my judicial duties. When I opened the door, my AA was there.

"All rise," she said, and the rest of her words faded into the distance as the proximity between me and Lucy grew smaller. She kept her eyes down. Even when she addressed the court, they never turned fully on me. A part of me wondered if she'd moved on. If there was someone else in her life. In her bed.

After appearances, I asked for the State's position. Lucy stood.

"Your honor. The State would be opposed to this child returning home. I understand that the Department of Children and Families is recommending the child return home, and we find this very concerning. It is the State's belief that the parents need additional therapy as well as continued individual therapy for the respondent. The child's health improved when removed from the home. Why would we put her back in the home for the possibility of continued neglect? The state would ask for a review in sixty days."

"Guardian ad lietem?" I asked.

"Thank you, Judge. I agree with the state, but the GAL would simply request that if the child returns home that DCF continue their supervision to insure the health of the child. The child does want to return to her parents' home, Judge."

"Mr. Watson?"

"Clearly, Judge, Mother is opposed to the child remaining in custody. She has completed her parenting classes, submitted to UAs, fulfilled the case plan in its entirety and is eager to have her daughter home. We would ask that this case be dismissed and jurisdiction be terminated."

I saw Lucy fidgeting in her seat. And I knew that my ruling would not make her happy. So far, I hadn't ruled against her...I mean, the State. She'd made great arguments and deserved those decisions.

"The court is going to find that Ms. Engle has completed the case plan, and though I'm not terminating jurisdiction, the court is ruling that the child return home to her mother. The court will set a review date, and a report from DCF needs to be prepared for the Court a week prior to that date. Is there anything further to come before the court?"

Lucy shot upright. "Your Honor, with all due respect, the State vehemently disagrees with this decision and requests Your Honor to take some time to take the decision under advisement. Perhaps a continuance."

"Thank you, Ms. Edwards, but the decision has been made. If there is nothing further, this matter is in recess."

With hooded eyes, I glanced toward Lucy. She stacked her folders with a clenched jaw. I wanted to explain, to tell her why but I stood and walked out of the courtroom. Her words 'why do you have to be so mean' resonated in my head. When I got to my desk, a note from Sara, my AA, let me know she had left early, something about her sick infant. Relief settled through me. I didn't want anyone to see my reaction to seeing Lucy. I collapsed in my chair.

Jesus. Why did I feel like shit? Judge Eichman was a friend more than a co-worker. I considered calling him for a possible reassignment as I rubbed my eyes with the heel of my hands. I rubbed so hard, I saw stars behind my lids. And, once I rested my head back against my chair and opened my eyes, I saw Lucy standing in front of me.

Her face was red, not flushed like after an orgasm, but fire red. Angry.

"Yes, Ms. Edwards?"

"Seriously, Your Honor. With all due respect, I strenuously disagree with that decision. Please, hear me out."

She paused to take a breath, so I sat back and gave her my undivided attention. She deserved that at the very least. What I wanted to do was bury myself inside of her as I bent her over my desk. Fighting that image, I folded my arms across my chest.

The most beautiful eyelashes fluttered as she appeared to gather her thoughts.

"Judge. That little girl, Paige, suffers from Munchausen Syndrome by proxy. Do you understand what that is?"

A smile nipped at the corners of my mouth, but the last thing I wanted was to disrespect her. But damn, she was cute.

"Yes, Miss Edwards. It's when you take your child to different doctors for made up illnesses and maybe have unnecessary procedures done. I understand it is a form of child abuse."

She shot her index finger in my direction. "NO! I mean, no, Judge. I mean, that's part of it. But…the parent or caregiver can actually make the child ill. They do things to make the child sick so that the doctors take them seriously. They inject them with things. They give them things orally."

The fight in her was endearing. And sadly, since she said the word orally, the only thing going through my mind was the way her mouth fit perfectly around my cock.

"Are you even listening, Judge?"

I cleared my throat. "Of course, I'm listening. Thank you for explaining the mental illness better. How does it pertain to the case at hand?"

The beautiful green eyes that I loved looking down at nearly popped out of her head. "How does it pertain to this case?" Her voice actually shot up several octaves. "You just sent a child home to a mother that makes her sick. I understand that the way you see it is the mother met the conditions of the case plan, but please look at the other side!"

The tone of her voice bordered on disrespectful, and there was no way in hell I'd have tolerated this from anyone else. No one.

"And what IS the other side, Miss Edwards?"

"The child only got better when removed from the home. You seem to think it's because this worthless piece of shit mother met some condition on her case plan. When in reality, the child got well when away from her mother!" she screamed.

"Watch your tone, Lucy," I gritted through clenched teeth.

"I won't watch my tone, Jenner." She clenched right back, surprising me. "That little girl was put right back in harm's way today. You put her in the hands of someone who hurts her." Her voice cracked, and the tears that pooled in her eyes quicker than I could realize spilled over onto her cheeks.

I swallowed my professional shit chased by my pride and stood to go to her.

"You don't understand," she whispered, then spun around and stormed out of my office.

By the time I got around my desk and across my office, the door to my division had closed. This wasn't a place I could chase her. All

I could do was pace. Back and forth. My heart pounded in my chest. Unleashing my anger and frustration, I kicked the wood door going into the courtroom, pain shot up my leg.

I fought to control what was happening inside of my chest. I didn't know she was going to cry, so I hadn't been prepared, but I knew it was something I never wanted to see again. Why did I fucking care if she cried? It didn't matter. It did. I wanted to go to her. To make things better. Jesus. I dragged my hand down my face. Bottom line, I fucked her and now it as over. But the feeling in my chest told me I was the one who was fucked. Personally and professionally.

LUCY

The best thing about living next to a baker…the smell. The smell of everything good.

When I got home, Midge saw my tear-streaked face and asked no questions. She simply enveloped me in a much-needed hug, overwhelming my nose with the smell of sweets and happiness.

When a knock sounded on my door a little while later, I had no doubt it was her. I met her with a half-hearted smile. Of course, her hands were full of baked goods as she made her way to my kitchen.

"I have lemon bars, rice crispy treats—which you know I don't believe are baked goods, but I know you like them—and a small tier wedding cake."

"Midge! You seriously made a wedding cake?"

As she set her gorgeous confections on my table, a smile a mile wide swept over my face. Flowers and baked goods did that for people.

She swatted her hand in the air. "Oh please, honey. It's a small tier with simple white frosting. Piece of cake, literally." She smiled. "But I know it's your favorite."

She was right. It was my favorite. Every year my Pops and Mimi celebrated their anniversary with a small, one tier wedding cake. And the three of us would eat it together. Wedding cake was the absolute best.

"Thank you. Thank you so much."

"Darlin', only one thing could cause those sorts of tears and chances are it has a penis. If he makes you cry, then he ain't worth it."

I threw her a silly grin. As much as I loved her and as much as I appreciated what she baked for me, I just wanted to be alone.

"Turn on a lamp in here," she said as she walked through the living room. "Light is good. Dark is…well, it's dark."

As she stood at the front door, she zapped me with the tea towel that draped over her shoulder. "And don't eat all those sweets. It'll make you fat, and you look beautiful just the way you are," she joked as she opened the door. "Oh! Excuse me," she added.

I peered around her to see Jenner standing in the hallway, wet from the storm outside. Midge's face hardened when she saw my reaction.

"Lucy? I have a rolling pin that I can fetch real quick."

Jenner didn't smile. He didn't laugh. His somber eyes focused only on me.

I tried to smile, but it never reached my face. "I'm ok, Midge. Thank you."

When she disappeared behind her door across the hall, Jenner stepped fully into my doorway. A haunted look clung to his eyes. The slump to his shoulders was indicative of his mood.

"Judge, come in," I tried to say, but the words wedged in my throat.

I'd not seen him quite like this. Sweat shorts, t-shirt, tennis shoes, soaked to the bone. Rain dripped off the ends of his sopping hair. A puddle collected at his feet.

My apartment was small enough that I only had to round a corner to grab him a towel. When I handed it to him, he cleared his throat and said, "Thank you."

I couldn't believe he was standing in my apartment. "How did you find me? New York is a pretty big place."

A sarcastic huff came out his mouth. "Yep. To be exact, there are seventy-two thousand people per square mile in Manhattan and five hundred people in that damn club and yet, I meet the one woman that I can't get out of my head and the one I also can't fucking have."

The words sent a tingling sensation fanning out across my chest that then spiraled down into my lower abdomen. He towel dried his hair, but his clothes still dripped on my rug.

"Do you see the irony in this?" he asked with his lips pulled tight.

I didn't answer. I assumed the statement was rhetorical. But I understood perfectly what he meant. All along I had cursed the cruel hand I'd been dealt. Our connection, our chemistry was off the charts from the beginning. All I wanted originally was a one-night hook up. This…whatever this was…hadn't been in the cards for me or so I thought. And yet, here we stood trying to figure it out.

"Tell me what I don't understand," he said.

"Pardon me?"

"When you left my office crying, you said I don't understand. Make me."

"Do you want some dry clothes first?"

"Do you have something that would fit?"

In my bedroom, I grabbed him the only pair of big, baggy sweats I had. When he came out of the bathroom, he was shirtless. The sweats, though baggy on me, fit him tighter.

"Do you have a dryer?"

Trying not to look at the curves of his chest or the abs that he no doubt worked hard for, I took the clothes and tossed them into the dryer. Over the past few hours, I'd made myself some mental promises that were becoming increasingly harder to keep.

"Would you like a drink?"

"No. Alcohol needs to stay out of this equation."

"You and your equations, Judge."

A slight smile touched his lips. "Don't call me Judge, Lucy. Not now. Not here." His eyes bore into me.

Neither of us knew what to say. Words that typically came easily for both of us were now absent. "I know I said no to the drink, but damn that stuff on the table looks pretty good."

I grinned. "Oh my God. You have to taste her stuff."

We both moved closer to the table. "By her, you mean the lady who was willing to beat me to death with a rolling pin?"

"Yep. That's the one."

We both reached for the same Rice Krispy treat, and he chuckled as he pulled on his end and I pulled on mine until the bar separated with marshmallow stringing out between the two pieces.

"Mmm," he moaned, stirring something low in my abdomen. "That is so delicious and buttery."

"I know. I think she doubles down on the butter and marshmallow." Manners pushed aside, I licked my fingers, cleaning them of the stubborn stickiness.

"Why the wedding cake?"

"It's just the smallest tier she can make. She knows it's my favorite."

"What's the occasion?"

From my small kitchen, I grabbed a sharp knife and aimed it at him—then shot him my evilest of glares. "No occasion. It's because I came home crying."

The perfectly shaped brows pulled together creasing his forehead as he swallowed, watching me cut the cake.

"You have to try this."

"Oh I wasn't going to leave until I did."

I stopped in mid cut, thinking about those words, but then finished slicing through the confection. The sexual tension in the room wasn't as easy to slice.

Once I placed the cake on the plate, I cut it in half.

"I call the piece with the icing," he said, reaching for it. But I quickly grabbed for it too, both of us fighting for the iced layer. Our fingers mushed into the white cake, destroying the inch-thick piece I'd cut. We both laughed out loud, still fighting for whatever mutilated cake was still on the plate, when suddenly he grabbed my fingers and shoved them into his mouth.

The hysterical laughter faded quickly as his tongue circled my two fingers and he sucked the icing and smashed cake off my fingers. Desire replaced the amusement that had danced in his eyes a minute ago. The warmth of his mouth, the way his tongue tenderly cleaned my fingers.

He closed his eyes and pulled my fingers from his mouth. I felt the coldness of the air as he released my hand, not just on my fingers but also in my heart. He wiped his fingers on a napkin and rubbed his palms together.

"Tell me something about you. Anything. I don't care what it is. Knowing you like wedding cake and Rice Krispy treats is a start." He grinned.

I shrugged worried his mind would change any time. "Hmm. Well, I love Dr. Pepper too. My favorite animal is the beluga whale. I've never been on an airplane. I don't really want kids."

His grin turned into a full-blown smile. "Please. What woman doesn't want kids. I don't want children either, by the way."

"Really? Why?"

"The man that everyone thinks is so great—the right-wing conservative prick who sits on the bench in DC—wasn't exactly father of the year. I just don't really want to give it a try."

"Trust me, I get it." God, did I understand.

He'd nearly backed me against the counter and my skin hummed with our close proximity. The electrical current buzzing between us was unquestionable. His penetrating stare kept our eyes locked. I so very much wanted him to touch me.

"Tell me now, Lucy. Tell me what I don't understand about the Munchausen case." The softness in his tone soothed me.

I gave him a nod and went to wash my hands.

"Ok." Tucking my legs beneath me, I sat almost as far away from him as I could get without choosing a different room. "What I'm going to say, only a few people know. People close to me."

He sat quietly, so I continued.

"I'm a Munchausen case," I whispered, staring at the pattern in the rug. I didn't want to see his reaction. It shouldn't matter to me anyway. "My mother was educated. She was a pharmacist. She was an actress. The best. I was given medicine. All sorts of medicine. I took it because I trusted her. I didn't understand that it was making me sick. I thought she was trying to make me better."

God, I hated talking about this. I'd told the stories to school staff, social workers, counselors, police. It made me feel weak, like I'd done something wrong. Unable to stay seated, I walked to the window, watching the flashes of lightning flicker in the dark sky. He remained silent.

"I'd had every test known to man it seemed. Colonoscopy, cystoscopy, endoscopy…you name the scopy, I may have had it." I chuckled through the seriousness. "We switched doctors more than we switched houses at that point. One summer, I spent some time with my Pops on his farm, and I felt remarkably better. It was only for thirty days. Hardly any pills, no doctors and I felt great. But, when I went back home and Mom started me on the pills again, I realized even at 9 years old that something wasn't ok. I told a teacher and the rest is history."

"No," he said softly, and my eyes flashed to him. "You can't stop there. Tell me the rest."

"The rest isn't what you wanna hear, Jenner. You want me to tell you something to make you feel better about your decision? I can't do that. I would have possibly died had I remained with my mother. Thank God, the judge in the town I lived in understood the disease."

Within a matter of seconds, he shot upright and bee lined it across the room. In that moment, I lost all focus and my words died in my throat as I backed up a step. The window against my back held me up as my legs wobbled beneath me.

"You think I came here because I feel bad about my decision? I don't, Lucy. There is this little thing called evidence that you seem to forget about sometimes. I can't take into consideration how you might "feel" about something. I can only consider what is presented to me under evidence. Did you have a mental health diagnosis for this mother? Did you have something from doctors saying this girl is being harmed or abused? Was there a nurse stating the child had been mistreated? That's what I need in order to rule the way you'd prefer I rule."

I shoved him back so I could escape the closeness, but he grabbed my upper arm, denying my get away. "I'm sure doctors and nurses always know best, right?" I spat out.

"I didn't come here to admonish you, Lucy."

"If you're going to talk like a judge, then I'll continue to call you Judge, Your Honor." I scowled.

He released a long, slow breath. "I didn't come here to scold you."

"Why did you come?"

His brows pulled together, and his eyes grew impossibly dark.

"To see if you were ok. You left my office crying, and I needed to know."

His grip loosened on my arm, and though it fell to my side, I didn't step away from him.

"You could have texted, Jenner," I whispered.

"I don't text."

"Bullshit," I said beneath my breath. "You wanted to see me. You want to be near me as much as I want to be near you."

There was no confirmation or denial of my statement—only a simple silent stare. For several long minutes, we stood nearly toe-to-toe. Neither of us moved. I wasn't sure if either of us breathed or even blinked.

"What do you want, Jenner?"

When I saw his jaw tighten, my stomach ached, and I didn't want that ache transferring to my heart.

"What do I want? I want to know if the woman I met nearly two months ago is something worth losing my career over. Because I don't know the answer to that at the moment. I feel like everyone around me would say "no". But, you and I...we click. We have amazing chemistry. We seem to feed off each other in ways I've never felt before. You make me laugh. And the sex was great, to put it mildly. But, Lucy, I don't know you. You don't know me. I can't quit thinking about a stranger and that doesn't make sense to me. To risk everything we've accomplished..."

His words faded off. I was able to complete the sentence in my own head.

"Don't you think I get that? All I ever wanted was to be the person to help the kids. What I'm doing is exactly what I went to law school for, Jenner. Some attorney's want to be these...these... hot shot defense attorneys. Some want to be judges." I pointed at him. "No one, and I do mean no one, wants to be a child in need of care attorney. You know that. In the judicial system, we both know that is not where the money is. But you know what? I don't care. I don't want to lose that."

"I agree with that, Lucy. Regardless of our connection, our professional responsibilities must take priority."

"Exactly. And honestly, I don't at all like you as a judge; how the hell would I like you as a boyfriend?" I said it as a joke, hoping to lighten the mood, but I so wanted him to disagree with what I said.

When he unleashed that killer smile, tinged with a hint of sadness, it was more than I could handle. Throwing caution to the wind, as tenderly as I could, I laid my palms flat on his chest, wanting to touch him if only this one last time. A painful grimace twisted his face as if my hands burned his bare skin.

"Lucy," he said beneath his breath. "We both know what we should do. We know our obligations. Even as an attorney, you have the same damn code of professional responsibility as I do." His words were soft.

Defeat...resignation...whatever it was colored his tone. By his demeanor, I knew I could easily push him over the edge. I could feel him teetering. Part of me felt like he wanted that. Maybe then he could blame me. The look in his eyes swayed between yes and no.

Trying to respect him, I lowered my hands from the warmth and hardness of his body. They fell to my sides in defeat of their own.

"I appreciate you checking on me, tonight. Thank you," I said, the professional tone creeping back into my voice. Forcing myself to take a step back, I forced a smile.

Something in his eyes shifted as he breezed past me. I'd seen it before. Welcome back Mr. Hyde. I heard my dryer close, and when he came out, he was dressed in his own clothes.

"Thank you for the use of your dryer." He bent down to tie his shoes. "I'm truly sorry about what you endured at the hands of your mother. I'm glad you got out of there and someone protected you."

"Thank you, Judge." For all my good intentions, I couldn't help the passive aggressive Judge I tossed out.

His irritated eyes shot up to mine, then he strolled to the door. "Yep. This matter is adjourned," he said coldly. And with that, he closed the door behind him. Adjourned, my ass.

CHAPTER 9

BINDING PRECEDENT

Lucy

Getting to the facility wasn't easy. First the subway then the bus. But when I arrived, Pops' head was upright, and he seemed alert. My heart stood still waiting for the verdict. His roaming eyes caught sight of me about the same time as Hank's did. Recognition registered in Pop's seventy-seven year old eyes as my heart screamed with joy. The look in his eyes made that whole cumbersome trip worth it.

"Hi Pops!"

Hank winked at me and mouthed, "It's a good day."

"There's my little miss."

Pops' body was frail, but I hugged him as tightly as I could, knowing that the next time he might not let me. I inhaled deeply taking in his scent. I missed the smell of the farm that used to cling to his clothes. Hank too waited for his hug, which I gladly obliged.

The next hour was spent telling Pops all about law school, graduation and my new job because he had no recollection of previous conversations. Hank was right about it being a good day. It was a great day. I knew Pops wouldn't remember it the next time we visited.

Hank updated Pops on the farm, the crops and all the animals. Thank goodness Hank and his sons were tending to all of it. I did what I could, but most of the time it landed on them. Honestly, I hadn't been to the farm in so long. When Hank met us with the truck on market days, my friends and I would help him during the weekend famers' market, but that was all I could manage right now. Some of my best memories were playing with Hank's boys—they were more like brothers than anything.

"Pops, I forgot to tell you, I brought you a Butterfinger." I found the candy bar in my purse. His favorite.

"I don't even like Butterfingers," he spat out hatefully.

As Hank's gaze found mine, my heart sunk. Butterfingers were Pops' favorite.

"Ok, Pops. It's ok." I slid the candy bar back next to my wallet for next time. "You want to play chess?"

"I don't know how to play chess," he snapped. The meanness in his voice made me cringe.

"Yes, you do, Pops. Let's try." Desperation swam through my words as I situated the pieces on the board.

Hanks hands gently covered mine, which still gripped a pawn and a knight that I had yet to place on the board.

"Look at me, little miss," he said barely above a whisper.

By the time my eyes found his, tears spilled over.

The wrinkles around Hank's eyes showed every bit of his 74 years of age. I loved him as much as Pops…almost.

"We had him for a wee bit. It was a good day. Chess isn't what's important."

Nodding, I swiped away the tears as Hank kissed the top of my head.

"Nurse," Pops blurted, his tone now cordial.

Forcing a smile, I glanced at him. "Yes, sir? What can I get for you?"

"My granddaughter is coming today. Would you please tell me when she gets here?"

Unable to hold back the tears—the dam burst. "Of course," I cried while smiling the best I could. "I know how excited she is to see you. She loves you so much."

"I raised her, you know. She's my little miss. Someday she's going to take over my farm. Boy oh boy does she love it there."

"I'm sure she does."

Hank patted my back. "I've got him from here, Lucy. Sir, I'm going to take you back to your room, ok?"

The nurses had come to the farm for nearly two years. Hank and I agreed to do what we could to keep Pops at home. The assisted care helped, but the challenge only grew, until we couldn't give him the care he needed any more. The pain of watching this cruel disease rob him of his mind and memories sliced my heart into pieces. He'd been at the home for five months now.

Pops had always expected me to take over the farm, but I wanted to be in the city. To live the city life. I had followed my dream. That decision disappointed him…hurt him. I leaned in from behind, brushed a kiss over Pops' thin hair and sat back, wishing I could tell Pops about Jenner but knowing he would probably never meet him.

CHAPTER 10

JUDICIAL DISCRETION

Jenner

Six and a half hours of utilizing Google, making phone calls and requesting information from a district attorney's office in Sullivan County, I'd finally gotten my hands on the petition from when she was a little girl. I thumbed through the document. My eyes scanned the obligatory wording until the specifics of the case were revealed.

Mother, who will be referred to here out as Miss Heasten is a registered nurse. Father is Derek Edwards. There is no known native American heritage known at this time. The state alleges Miss Heasten was responsible for using a syringe for injecting respondent with various drugs including but not limited to opioids, barbiturates and various chemicals. Miss Heasten took the respondent to a variety of doctors named on the witness list for numerous unnecessary tests. The respondent reported her health issues and continued injections to a teacher at her school, Linda Wilson. DCF investigated and the respondent was given a urinalysis and blood test, which came back positive for multiple drugs. DCF removed the respondent from the home placing the respondent in police protective custody until....

With increasing irritation, I tossed the papers onto my desk, then laced my fingers and rested my forehead on my thumbs. Blood surged violently through my veins. I'd never have given her back to her mother either. How could she not see the difference in these cases? In her case, there was clear and convincing evidence.

"Judge, your conference begins in about two hours. You are completely registered and they are holding your registration. I told them you were running late."

"Thank you."

"I'm surprised you're still here. I cleared your schedule a month ago."

"I had some things I needed to take care of."

"Anything I can help with?" my assistant asked, handing me papers as I stepped past her.

"Nope. I've got what I need, for now. Thank you."

This conference was my worst nightmare. Three days of legislative updates, judicial reviews and legal bullshit. But it did get me out of the office for three days with no possibilities of seeing Lucy. Dragging myself away from her apartment was one of the hardest things I'd ever done. But, seeing her passion for what she did, the rationale behind her taking on child in need of care cases, and her pledge of loyalty to children—I knew I had to step away. Neither one of us could afford the fallout if I didn't. I wasn't scared of much in my life, but the thought of never touching her again, terrified me.

"Jenner! How are you?" Judge Williams greeted me in our first CJE credit.

"Hey, Peter. I'm good. Great to see you. Though drinks and cigars would be way better."

We both chuckled as we took our seats near the front of the auditorium because of our tardiness.

"Trust me, three days away from my wife is almost better."

I grinned. His words only made me think of Lucy. I couldn't imagine wanting to be away from her if she were mine.

"Maybe we can catch up with a drink tonight."

"That'd be great." I could certainly use a drink.

Four judges walk into a bar…I wasn't sure of the joke yet, but I was pretty sure there was one out there somewhere.

The four of us, dressed in khaki shorts and polo's and looking causally judicial, sat at a table in the half-full bar. I was obviously the youngest of the group. I knew when I started my judgeship that because of my father's judicial status my integrity would always be questioned. The credibility of my professional decisions would be closely monitored. Even though I didn't give a shit about the job, I still had a lot to prove.

A group of college-aged girls in the corner obnoxiously bellowed out a Garth Brooks hit completely off key. Judge Steve Bryant made some snide comment about getting one of the girls back to his room. He was a good twenty years older than all four of them. Plus, he looked about seven months pregnant. My guess was they might not even accept a drink from him, but I chuckled nonetheless.

When three more young women walked through the arch of the doorway, I only noticed because Steve made an 'mmm' sound like from a Campbell's soup commercial. When I shot a glance toward the girls to see what had caught his attention, Lucy's smiling face sent a punch straight to my gut. You've got to be fucking kidding me. Only 8.5 million people in this city. I quickly lowered my head, attempting to hide my reaction from my companions. Steve's continued boorish sounds like he was about to devour a meal shot my blood pressure high. There was no way to tell which woman elicited those lewd grunts, but I'd be damned if it was going to be Lucy.

She and her friends sat at a table opposite us with a few tables in between. She hadn't noticed me, but damn, I couldn't take my eyes off her. How the hell did she show up at the same bar? Pretty typical for our relationship. Hell, for my luck, if I up and traveled to Chicago, she'd probably be visiting Chi town as well. Fuck fate.

Excusing myself, I disappeared to the restroom. Seeing her, thinking about her hands on my bare chest earlier, any resolve I had made to let her go began to fade. I was banking on having hurt her enough when I told her we were adjourned that she would push me away. I needed her to be angry. Obviously, I couldn't count on myself to be the sensible one. I stared at my reflection in the water-spotted mirror, wondering if a

YOUR HONOR

second career option was out there. My three-day stubble was starting to itch. How had I forgotten to shave? A goatee wasn't totally acceptable in my career, but I was operating in the *I don't give a shit* mode.

Neil Diamond had replaced Garth's crooning when I strolled out of the restroom. Lucy's laugh rang out over the music, making me smile. Until I rounded the corner and saw Steve over talking to her. Then, I saw red.

LUCY

The bar across from the hotel was the perfect place to drink away the resounding memories of Jenner coursing through my mind. Enduring law school sexless had been a piece of cake compared to the daunting thought of never touching Jenner again. It was all I could do not to cover my ears when all the assistants in the office started gushing about how good looking he was and speculating about how hot it would be to kiss him. By the time Bethany, Hope and I went for a drink that evening, I was sick to death of the conference already, and it'd only been one day.

The music switched from Garth to Neil Diamond as we shot back another drink. For me, getting away wasn't as big of a deal as it was for others. I liked living alone and already had my fill of peace and quiet. But most of the people attending the conference couldn't wait to leave their spouses, kids or even parents.

A cool miniature train circled around the bar near the ceiling. It was obvious why the place was called The Rail. The front of a train engine sat center stage with the bar encasing it, and two cabooses near the back served as private rooms.

"Your boss is a bitch," Hope said into my hair leaning into me.

"Who?"

"Daryanne Watkins." She pointed across the bar at a beautiful blonde in what looked like an expensive suit who was tabbing out.

"That's my boss?"

"Yep. One of the chief DA's. Merciless. Wicked. I went to law school with her. I take it you didn't interview with her?"

"Nope but duly noted," I laughed.

75

"What are you girls drinking?" a guy from behind us asked.

I didn't even turn around. I wasn't interested in the slightest. I should be…to get my mind off of Jenner, but I wasn't. Both Bethany and Hope turned though. I'd have been content right then to go back to my hotel room and read. The girls told him what they were drinking.

"And you, lovely lady?" he asked, sidling closer to me. When I glanced at him, he looked nice enough. Bigger in the belly and definitely older than me by maybe fifteen or so years.

"I'm good. But, thank you."

"You girls seem too young to be judges, so I'm guessing attorneys?"

Bethany spun completely around to face him. "What on earth makes you think we are attorneys?"

"We are, BTW," Hope spat out, making me laugh.

"I'm assuming you walked over from the hotel," the man said. "I just thought four old judges could buy you ladies a drink, that's all."

My ears perked up. "There are judges at this conference?"

"Not just old ones."

A tingling sensation fluttered up my spine as Jenner's voice soaked slowly into my pores. I had no choice but to look at him.

"Judge Weber," I greeted with a half-hearted smile. A magnetic force drew our eyes to one another's.

"Hello, Miss Edwards. Out in the real world, you can call me Jenner. How are you?"

Hearing my name, even with all of his formality, made my heart skip a beat. "I'm tired, actually. Going to turn in soon. But good to see you. How are you?"

"I'm good as well. I'm not sure how much longer I'll be out either."

"Hello, Jenner. I'm Hope." She interrupted and nudged me with her elbow, then offered her hand to him.

"Hello, Hope."

His dark eyes flickered to hers as he shook her hand, then back to mine as an awkward silence fell between us.

"Trust me, Jenner, she's not going anywhere," Hope added. "We met some guys from Jersey in one of our sessions. They're supposed to meet us later."

Jenner's jaw ticked as his eyes flickered with something I couldn't read. I glanced toward the basketball game playing on one of the TVs at the bar.

"Ah-ow," the judge who offered to buy us drinks moaned out loud as he pretended to stab himself in the heart. "We've already been replaced... by attorneys." He laughed, and I flashed an exaggerated smile, trying to enjoy myself. My body hummed simply from Jenner's proximity.

His body shifted toward mine, transmitting a message only I would understand. No matter how many people stood around us, he, too, was thinking about what happened between us. The boundaries we'd crossed.

"LUCY! I'm home!" a deep voice from behind me shouted sounding like Ricky Ricardo. Before I could turn, Jenner's eyes abandoned mine, glaring at the young guys coming in the door.

When I spun around on the stool, I saw the guys from the Supreme Court update session. Advaith was the darker-skinned guy, but I couldn't recall which one was Kurt or which was Matt.

Offering them a smile, I waved. Hope stood and did the intros.

"These guys are judges," she laughed, pointing. "They are fraternizing with the peons." She winked at Jenner. Who wouldn't wink at Jenner?

"Judge Weber, Judge Bryant and Judge Kingsman."

"Weber?" Matt asked. "Any relation to the big guy down in Washington?" he laughed.

Everything inside of me cringed. This was so getting off on the wrong foot.

Jenner cleared his throat. "That 'big guy' is my father."

Matt's complexion turned three different shades of white as I grabbed a couple of dollars and escaped to the jukebox. I closed my eyes, holding onto the glass trying to breathe my way out of this. Then, without even opening them, I knew he was there. My body felt it.

"Seriously, you girls were meeting up with those guys?"

"Meeting up with them, Jenner. Not fucking them. And, why does that even matter?"

I pushed the numbers with force to play Beyoncé's Irreplaceable first. Then just as forcefully entered Cry me a River by Justin Timberlake. One song left. I went with I Knew You Were Trouble by T-Swift. Proud of my choices, I glanced up at him.

"They are tools." He gripped the front of the jukebox like he was ready to break the glass. "'Lucy, I'm home'?" Jenner mimicked Kurt. "You can't be serious."

"We met at the session today, chatted about having a drink. Don't make it more."

"Yes. And if I remember correctly, that's how you met me. Are you going to come around his finger tonight? Or are you just going to tie your shirt in a knot and call it quits?"

With pursed lips, I narrowed my eyes.

"Stop acting like a jealous boyfriend, Your Honor."

With that, I spun around and headed back to the table.

About an hour had passed with Jenner's eyes burning into me for the first half hour of it. For the last thirty minutes, he and Hope had been discussing a legal issue with her apartment. I wasn't normally the jealous type. The only jealously I'd ever experienced was that of kids who had both parents or even one who came to their events and graduations. But, sitting there watching Jenner and Hope engage in conversation, I had to admit that the irritated buzz in the back of my head grew with every passing minute. He could take her back to his room if he wanted and have his way with her. She worked for a private firm and would never be anywhere near his courtroom. They wouldn't have any issues with a relationship. So, who was the jealous one? I sipped my drink faster than I should.

"Sorry to interrupt, Judges," Kurt drawled. "But ladies, you ever had a key party?"

Bethany shook her head. "Nope." Her eyes looked hazed over. "Tell us how to play."

Kurt held up his hotel key card and then pointed to his two friends, who also sported key cards. "We all three put our keys in the center of the table. Each of you pick a key. No one knows who they got until we get to the hotel." Kurt relaxed back in his chair, looking proud.

"Jesus," Jenner muttered, shaking his head and downing the amber liquid in his tumbler.

"Does that shit really work?" Judge Bryant asked the younger boys.

"Of course it does," Matt said laughing.

My phone chimed, and I grabbed it. When I saw Jenner's name on my screen, my heart stalled.

My key is the only key you'll leave here with.

Unsure if his eyes were on me, I tried to steady my breathing as I typed back.

I thought you didn't text. But. Is that a proposition?

I kept my phone in my hand. Jenner stood and excused himself. The other two judges shook their heads. Momentarily, my phone buzzed.

No. But you are damn sure not accepting one of theirs.

With him still in the restroom, I clutched my purse and decided to leave.

"Hey girls, my head is killing me," I lied. "Not sure why. Tomorrow night, we drink. Deal?" My words came out quickly.

"No! Don't go."

"I'm know. I'm sorry. Gonna head to my room."

Kurt held up his room key. "Or my room, Lucy," he laughed.

I shook my head, laughing at his eagerness. Jenner reappeared at the table, trying not to posture, but failing miserably. I was the only one who really noticed as I strolled past him. As the door closed behind me, I saw him glance down at his phone.

CHAPTER 11

JUDICIAL ACTIVISM

Lucy

The night air was cooler than when we'd come in. Glad I had thrown on my jean capris, I wished I'd worn my sweater. Swarms of people walked the streets. Even in the business district, there were enough bars and restaurants to make this area fun in the evening. A group of girls all decked out for a bachelorette party laughed on the street corner. Dildo necklaces circled their necks, and the bride carried a dildo cup. I laughed as I walked past them, listening to their slurred, drunken words.

I cast a glimpse back toward the bar door, wondering if Jenner had followed me, but I didn't see him. Images of him and Hope talking battered my brain. My bi-polar thoughts drove me crazy.

The crosswalk pedestrian signal began the countdown for me to walk. Hustling across the street, I just wanted to get back to my room, away from him. I stopped at the hotel bar and ordered a glass of wine, putting it on my room tab. I wasn't much of a drinker, but I hated beer and hated even more the fruity crap that a lot of girls drank. Wine I could do…and a dirty martini.

As the elevator moved slowly up, I stared out the glass into the lush courtyard of the hotel. My eyes didn't spot what they searched for before the elevator dinged at my floor. When the doors opened, I took a sip of my drink and stepped off—and there he was.

The wine stuck in my esophagus mid swallow. I cleared my throat.

"You left the bar because of me?" he asked.

How in the hell had he beat me back? "Yes." I moved past him. "Careful, Judge. Someone may see us talking." A sarcastic pitch hung in my tone.

"Lucy." Something lingered in his tone as well.

I scanned my key over the pad on my door, which flashed green, unlocking the door. I pushed it open, releasing it and silently listening for him to catch the door. After I dropped my purse in the corner, I turned around, staring at him.

"What do you want, Judge." I hoped my calling him judge annoyed him. "We didn't swap keys. So, why are you standing in the door of my hotel room?"

A grimace flickered over his facial features, but he remained silent.

"Pleading the fifth? What the hell happened to this matter is fucking adjourned?" I asked. His back and forth on whatever "we" were was exhausting, and every single time he found me, my hopes grew higher.

"Watch your mouth, Lucy."

Holding on to the stem of the wine goblet, I gulped the red wine until it was gone. "You're not my father, Jenner."

"No. I'm not. Not even close."

My eyes snapped to meet his. He knew something about my father. His words held a knowing comparison. Shit. I didn't want him to know anything. Embarrassment caused me to ignore the comment.

He shook his head, still standing with both hands in his pockets.

"Why did it matter to you if I went to one of those guy's rooms?" I asked, hoping to back him into an admission.

"You mean besides them being complete douche bags?"

"Yes, besides that."

"Is that what you wanted, Lucy? One of them?"

"You know that's not what or who I wanted, Jenner."

Before I totally finished my sentence, he raked his fingers through his hair. My phone rang from my purse, but I ignored it. Nothing was going to interrupt us. He took a seat on the corner of my bed. His silence crushing.

"What is wrong with you? Say something!" I raised my voice, turning away and staring out the high-rise window.

"Say something? What do you want me to say, Lucy? Do you want me to read you the oath I took? There was a little part about faithfully and impartially discharging and performing all duties…" He sighed. "That's the part I'm struggling with. I rule against you one time, and you come to my chambers to argue. I cannot let personal bias get in the way of my decisions. What part of that is confusing to you?"

"I needed you to understand that you made the wrong decision in that case," I explained.

"You never would have gone to chambers had it been a different judge. You came to my chambers because of the relationship we have. I can't be impartial when it comes to you. I…can't."

My heart swelled and cracked all at the same time. I would never feel his hands on my body again, I just knew it. "I took an oath too, you know."

"Yes. But I'm the judge, Lucy. I'm held to a higher standard. I'm the one that has to say no. I'm the one that has to back down. I'm the one who has to draw the line."

"And that's just so simple for you?"

"It damn well should be. But would I really be standing in your hotel room desperately wanting to touch you if it was that simple?"

The professional and ethical dilemma we found ourselves in was brutally unfair. Quit our jobs. Quit each other. Unjust options.

"Just go, Jenner. It's fine. I get it."

"You don't get it. I've been trying to get myself to leave this room since the moment I stepped in, and I can't leave to save my life, Lucy, let alone my career."

Our eyes locked as a long minute ticked, the sexual tension almost stifling. It was like the low hum of a power substation—always there.

My phone started ringing again. Something was wrong. It was too late at night for me to just coincidentally get two calls within ten minutes. I grabbed it from my purse. Hank.

"I have to answer this," I explained. "Hank? What's wrong?" I turned to face the window again, needing to find an ounce of concentration. Hank never called this late.

"Hey, Little Miss. Where are you?"

"Hank. Just tell me. What's wrong?"

"Well now, I need you to relax because he's gonna be just fine. But Pops took a tumble tonight," Hank clarified. "They called me just a bit ago.

"Where are you?" I snatched my purse up so fast half the contents fell out of it. Tears pooled in my eyes as I bent down to pick the stuff up.

"We're at the hospital just to make sure that he didn't mess up his squash," Hank chuckled.

Suddenly, Jenner was next to me, touching my hands, pushing them away from the things that had spilled. He picked up all my personal things and slid them into my purse. While Hank told me where to go, Jenner got his car keys out of his pocket, grabbed my sweater and stood at the door with my purse in his hand. That's when the tears spilled over.

JENNER

When she disconnected the call and followed me out of the room, she didn't seem to even know which way to go.

"Lucy," I said taking her hand. "Come on." I directed her to the elevator unsure myself where we were going, but knowing I'd take her there. "Will you tell me what's going on?"

She swiped away the tears from her cheeks nodding. "Yes. But you don't have to do this. I can catch a cab to the hospital. Seriously."

"Don't be ridiculous. Please, tell me what's happened."

"My Pops. The man that raised me. He's my grandpa. He fell tonight," she cried, and without thinking, I pulled her close. Intimacy felt right with her. And her god damned body fit perfectly into my side. Though my brain cussed me once we were close. It was like handing a hypodermic needle to a heroin addict.

No sooner did I hold her close to me than the elevator doors slid open, exposing us. Four people waited to get on as we instinctively pulled apart. I silently hoped she forgave me for letting go.

In the car, I stared at her, speechless as soundless tears streaked her beautiful face. I'd seen her cry from anger or frustration, but this was from hurt. I shook my head, irritated with myself as my heart melted, wanting to hold her, to comfort her. All I could do was take her shaking hand in mine.

She caught me staring, but I didn't look away. I hadn't been able to show her that I cared; I desperately wanted her to know now. Yet, all I offered her was a tight-lipped smile. I truly was an emotional cripple.

"How did you know about my father?"

My eyes suddenly clung to the road, watching every curve approach and following the lines. Where before I couldn't take my eyes off of her, now I couldn't meet her gaze. I had told myself that my research into her past was so that I could understand what had happened with her mother… how that made Lucy the way she was…but I realized it was more than that.

"I read about him."

"Why?"

After an extremely long minute, I lied. "I wanted to review how the judge ruled in your case. How he managed to get you out of the home."

Her forlorn eyes left mine and gazed out at the road. It wasn't a total lie. I did, in fact, want to judicially review the case. But that's not why I made the request for her file.

"A crazy mother and a criminal father. Pretty impressive, eh?" Her voice cracked, and I squeezed her hand.

"We aren't our parents, Lucy. Your father robbed banks. He didn't harm people. Regardless, that doesn't mitigate what I feel for you."

Her lips parted at that admission, and her green eyes rounded.

Before my mouth betrayed me more, I lifted her hand to my lips and brushed the soft skin with a kiss. The hospital was still another ten minutes away, but we spent that time in silence.

The emergency department was crowded with people. Generally, just by looking, you could tell who was sick and who was waiting. Given that flu season had just begun—this wasn't the best time to be in a place like this. I prowled behind Lucy as her eyes scanned the rooms for familiar faces. When she bee lined it for a corner, I followed closely. An older gentleman stood when he saw her.

"Hank," she cried, latching onto him.

"Hey now, Little Miss. He's gonna be just fine. But I think he has a broken rib."

She quickly pushed away from the man and greeted the man in the wheelchair.

"Hey, Pops," she whispered, touching his shoulder.

"Yes, ma'am. Is my granddaughter here? I need her to know that I fell."

Lucy nodded. "Yes, sir," she answered, crippling me with confusion. "She is crazy with worry and told me to tell you how much she loves you," she cried as the Hank guy rubbed her back.

Perplexed, I touched Hank's arm, trying to draw his attention.

"Can you tell me if he's been seen yet?"

"No, sir. You came with Lucy?"

I nodded. "Yes, sir." I wasn't sure who this guy was, but he seemed important to her. "Will you excuse me?"

Scrolling through my contacts, I hit Bryce Boyles. After three rings, he answered.

"Jenner, what's up, buddy?"

"Hey, Bryce. I need a favor."

"Sure, what's up?"

"We are in the ER and I need someone seen ASAP." I glanced behind me to where Lucy was coming apart in Hank's arms. His worn hands brushed down the back of her hair.

"Jenner?"

"Yeah. Sorry. What'd you say?" I'd missed Bryce's comment.

"What's the name?"

"It's Jack Walker. He's an elderly man that fell tonight. I know it's not life threatening. But he needs x-rays."

"Of course. I'll call in now. Not sure who the ER doc is tonight, but I got you, man."

"Thanks, man. I appreciate it. I owe you one."

"We both know you owe me more than one."

I smiled as I disconnected the call.

Lucy sat in a chair as worry etched creases in her forehead. Hank sat next to her. There were no empty seats near her, so I sat next to a window and watched her fiddle with her phone.

You ok? I texted.

First, she glanced at her screen, then up until our eyes met.

I will be. Thank you for bringing me.

You're welcome. I have a question.

?

I assumed her one question mark was the go ahead for me to ask.

Does your Pops have dementia?

After I hit send, I looked over at her. I watched as she opened my text. Her entire face crumbled. She glanced up at me trying to hide the raw emotion, but when she nodded, two tears trickled down her cheeks. *Jesus*, I whispered beneath my breath. This poor girl had been dealt the shittiest of hands. It no longer mattered to me who saw us, I needed to go to her. So I did.

Despite the mass of people, she stood as if reading my mind, as I rounded the corner, stepping around folks to get to her. From my peripheral vision, I saw Hank watching me. The moment I got to her, I enveloped her with my arms, lifting her so that her feet dangled. I wanted to carry her burden, to somehow give her a break.

She buried her face in my shoulder. Neither of us spoke; I just wanted her to know I was there for her. I'd hold her for as long as she held onto me.

"Jack Walker?"

Her body stiffened as she shifted around, and I allowed her feet to touch the ground. She wiped her face with both hands and sniffed. She needed a Kleenex, and I didn't have one.

"Are you Judge Weber?" the doctor in scrubs asked.

"Yes." I reached to shake his hand.

"Bryce called. Is this the gentleman?"

"Yes, sir," Lucy stepped forward. "He fell."

"OK. Why don't you bring him back, and we'll get him into X-ray."

Lucy turned to me before she walked off and whispered thank you.

Two cups of coffee, three email checks, five out dated magazines and a couple of hours later, Lucy strolled out when the electronic door slid open. I'd watched that door all night waiting for a glimpse of her. Her tired eyes spotted me as her brows pulled together.

"Jenner. You're still here?" she seemed surprised.

I stretched my body as I stood to greet her; my knees cracked in complaint. "Of course, I am. I'm your ride." I winked at her. "What's the verdict with your grandfather?"

"Broken collar bone and a rib."

"Damn. How's he doing?"

She tried to hide a yawn. "They're keeping him overnight. Keeping an eye on his lungs. He's low on iron and potassium."

"You ready, Little Miss?" Hank asked, coming through the door then spotting me.

"If you don't mind, Hank, I'd like to take her." He and I hadn't officially met so I extended my hand. "I'm Jenner, by the way."

Hank shifted his posture to give Lucy a cautious look. I made a mental note to ask her about that later. But, he did shake my hand. His handshake was strong and heavy. "Well, Jenner, I reckon Lucy needs to decide who she rides with."

She laid her head against Hank's chest. "I love you. I'll see you tomorrow." Then she tiredly walked toward me. Despite my inner joy that she chose me, I respectfully nodded to Hank, an unspoken reassurance that I'd take care of her—at least for tonight.

CHAPTER 12

JUDICIAL RESTRAINT

Lucy

"Lucy," Jenner whispered, gently shaking me awake. The yellow lights from the parking garage shone through the windshield. "We're at the hotel."

"Oh my goodness. I'm sorry. I fell asleep," I said, peeling my eyelids apart.

"Please don't apologize. I know you're tired."

Jenner rested his hand comfortably at the small of my back. I wanted more than anything to invite him to my room, but I knew what his response would be. No sense going through the agony again.

"Thank you for staying tonight."

"Lucy. I was your ride. I wasn't going to leave you."

Those obligatory words didn't offer much comfort.

Silence always seemed to find its way between us, this time it was in the elevator. This undeniable connection between us really had no explanation. Jenner was right. We didn't even know each other. Not really. So why was it so hard to accept the impossibility of our situation? Why couldn't we just say goodbye and mean it? I was too emotionally exhausted at this point to try to sort it all out.

Once we made it to my room, he used my key card to open the door and then followed me inside. I stood watching as he turned down the bed.

I knew what I was about to ask was unfair. Stupid in fact. But I didn't care.

"You'll stay with me?" I asked, knowing I was pressuring him. Hating myself for it.

I saw his eyes close and heard his heavy exhale. "Is that what you want, Lucy?"

Feeling his resilience fade, I quietly whispered, "Please. Just for tonight. Hold me."

Neither of us spoke after that. He stripped down to his boxer briefs. I stripped down too, more uncomfortable now than I had been before with him. This was different than after the club that night. I didn't know him then…there were no expectations. But everything changed after that fateful day in court. I grabbed the white undershirt he'd taken off and slid it over my head before taking off my bra.

He lifted the covers for me, and when I crawled in, I scooted until my back was against his chest. His body swallowed mine as he draped a leg over me and wrapped one arm around my ribs, tucking me snuggly to him. This was a first for me. I'd never slept in bed with a man. I expected to feel claustrophobic, instead I felt blanketed in safety.

"One night," he whispered. "One night. Sleep tight, Little Miss."

I smiled to myself. I'd take one night. I think…

I knew before I fell asleep that he'd be gone when I woke up…and he was. A handwritten note rested on the nightstand. He wouldn't text but he was the king of handwritten notes.

L- You have no idea the super hero strength it required to lay next to you for even a short night and not touch you. 317-743-9917—this is the number to Dr. Shu. He's taken over your grandfather's case. I spoke to him this morning. Mr. Walker did well overnight. Doctor is expecting your call. If you don't mind texting me to let me know if you're doing okay, I'd appreciate it. J

I fell back onto the bed. Damn that man…I didn't know much about Jenner Weber—but there were a few things I was sure of. We were in for one hell of a battle. I'd worked my entire life to earn my law degree, so I could do what I'd dreamed of, to protect as many children as I could. Yet, one man stood in the way of that—he wasn't just a judge; he was the man I had fallen for. Hard.

I saw no sign of Jenner the entire day. The doctor who had miraculously been assigned to Pops' case was texting me updates. Very unconventional. My guess was Jenner had a hand in my preferential treatment. My phone buzzed during my afternoon session, and this time it was Jenner.

I'm hoping you are awake by now. And I'm hoping that you haven't been trapped under something heavy preventing you from texting. #ihatetexting

I grinned at his hashtag, glancing up at the dull PowerPoint presentation then back to my phone. Hope slid a sheet of paper in my direction. I texted him back:

I made it to my 9 am session! #notaslacker #thenwhydidyoutellmetotext

I giggled to myself then read what Hope had written.

We are meeting the judges and attorneys tonight. We saw them at breakfast before you came down. Just FYI.

I assumed by judges she meant Jenner? I hand wrote back:

By judges, you mean the ones from last night? Why?
My phone buzzed again. Jenner.

I've taken judicial notice of your work ethic, Miss. Edwards. I'm

90

not sure of your sleeping patterns or your personal leave usage so the verdict is still out on the slacking part. I asked you to text because I was interested in knowing how your grandfather was doing. #iamacaringman

Hope shoved the paper back my way. But, I responded to Jenner first.

Caring man? You sent a child home to a mother that's going to hurt her. Kidding. Sort of. Pops is doing ok. Keeping him another day. Going by after conference today. #whenyoucareyouaresupposedtoshowit

I grabbed the paper from Hope.

Yes those judges. The one you work for is freaking hot. Since you can't fuck him, set us up.

My heart sunk as I watched her scratch out the words, then wink at me. In the mean time, my phone buzzed from the man she wanted to fuck.

Yes, I spoke to Dr. Shu. Need a ride? #seehowcaring

Let me get this straight, Your Honor. You can violate federal HIPAA laws by talking to a friend about my grandfather but you must not violate your judicial code??? #youcantpickandchoose

My phone buzzed almost immediately.

Delete your texts and this will be discussed later #ihatetextingx2

I bit down on my lip as the fear of teasing gone too far weighed on me. And I only felt worse when I glanced at the paper Hope and I had been exchanging messages on. He wasn't even mine, but the thought of someone else having him made my stomach churn.

91

The strong smell of disinfectant and bleach whirled through my nose as I sat in Pops' room where he had slept soundly for the past two hours. To me, he seemed frailer than before. Even weaker than when I last saw him at the home. The skin on his bruised hands was loose…thin. As I rubbed over the bruised skin with my fingers, I thought about the countless times those hands had fixed me up with his first aid kit. After the court placed me with Pops, he went far above what was necessary to make me feel loved and protected. I always wanted to do the same when our roles were reversed.

When I went off to college, Hank moved in with Pops full time. Maggie, Hank's wife, had died years earlier too. Pop and Hank had worked together in the fields and in the garden keeping the farm running smoothly until two years ago. Pops always had big, calloused, muscular hands—true farm hands. And as I dragged my fingertips over the backs of them, it struck me how only a shell of those hands remained.

I lay back in the chair, closed my eyes and thought about Pops' hand gripping Jenner's in a firm handshake. The reality of Pops ever seeing me with any man was slim but God, how I would love that.

"Hey. Little Miss. Wake up."

When my eyelids pulled apart, Hank stood over me, shaking my shoulder. My eyes immediately fell onto Pops. He was sitting upright staring at the TV. Anxiously, I stared up at Hank. The frown on his face was all I needed.

"Go back to your hotel and get some sleep. It's after nine."

"Nine!" I shot upright. I'd slept for nearly four hours. Who sleeps for four hours, especially in a hospital?

"I'll call you if we need you," he smiled, leaning in for a hug.

Feeling his arms was almost as good as Pops' arms.

I went straight to the bar that Hope and Bethany had texted about. It was on the opposite side of the hotel in an area that wasn't as busy. The last text from the girls certainly got my attention. *Your judge is sexy af.*

Walking from the subway to the bar, I looked down at my sweat shorts and Cubs long-sleeved shirt. I must look like an idiot out in shorts at almost ten at night this close to winter. I seriously didn't care what I looked like. Even after my mid-evening nap, I felt exhausted. If I went to the hotel room to change, I'd crash again. I had no doubt. And, I wasn't about to leave Jenner alone with Hope.

The bar was loud, and Kurt was the first one to see me as he eagerly waved me over. I was under dressed to say the least. Some guys were in ties, some in sport coats, but no one had on sweat shorts, least of all the girls who were dressed in heels similar to my attire that first night I met Jenner in the club. I caught a glimpse of my gray Nikes in a mirror as I walked to their table. Kurt wasn't the only one watching me walk across the bar; it seemed all eyes followed me to the table, as my clothing screamed outsider.

"Damn, Luce. You dressed up for us," Bethany laughed.

"Clearly. I came straight from the hospital."

"How's your grandpa?"

I nodded. "He's doing ok. Where is everyone?" And by everyone, I meant Jenner.

"Hope and Judge Weber are over playing shuffle board. Kurt and I were playing pool, but we lost to those two douche bags." Matt and Advaith grinned.

I plopped my booty up on a bar chair where I could creep on Jenner and Hope with my peripheral vision. They looked like they were a team playing another couple. My heart sunk a bit.

Kurt slid a dirty martini my way. "I remembered," he said, tapping his temple.

"Thank you," I smiled.

"I was wondering if we could chat about a case," he asked.

"Of course. What's up?" I loved talking about cases. I loved the thought of helping a child. You know how a parent loves their child before they even meet them? That was me—saving them, helping them. That's what I was born to do. Funny how I wanted none of my own.

"It's a case you filed about thirty days ago. The parents hired me as counsel."

"Oh, cool. Which one?"

"Hunting. Jeff Hunting."

"Three year old. Yes, I remember. He was found at 2 am in a local market. No parent. No shoes."

Kurt sipped his drink. "Allegedly."

"Allegedly, my ass," I laughed. "I've got witnesses and police statements."

My martini was going down smoothly…and quickly.

"Fair enough. I was going to see if you would be open to doing an Order of Informal Supervision. These parents want to comply."

"HA!" I laughed. "They were high on meth, Kurt. Do you know what meth does? It makes you not responsible enough to care for your children. Hence the middle of the night trip for the toddler to the grocery market."

He nodded. "I agree. But the child was in foster care for seven days. They've learned their lesson."

Eating my green olive, I chewed on what he said. I wasn't sure selfish parents like that could learn a lesson.

"I suppose if you buy me another drink, we could discuss conditions," I winked playfully.

"Done."

Halfway through my second martini, Hope and Jenner came back to the table. Even though Kurt was talking, I watched her touch Jenner's bicep through his polo.

"I tell you what." I tried to focus on Kurt. "You have both parents get a drug and alcohol assessment, submit to UA's, and allow Family Preservation into their home, and I'll be much more willing to consider it."

Kurt leaned in close to me. "Deal. I can think of a few other conditions we could tie in." He slid a cocktail napkin toward me. He'd written in black ink:

Love your brains. Love your body more. 516-244-7911

I glanced up at him with raised brows, not knowing how to respond to that. How did we go from attorney/attorney conversation to him liking my body?

"Hey girlie. How's your grandpa?" Hope asked.

I nodded. "He's doing ok. How are you?"

"I'm good." Hope held up her index finger and thumb measuring about an inch. "I'm a wee bit drunk," she whispered. "Still hoping to score with the hot judge."

I smiled…on the outside.

"Oh my!" she squealed. "Who gave you their number?" Hope snatched the napkin waving it in the air.

My eyes darted to Kurt, then to Jenner. His glossy eyes stared past me at Kurt. When Kurt's phone started ringing on the table, he grabbed it quickly but it was too late.

"Ah, ha!" Hope shouted. "Kurt likes Lucy." Then she tossed the napkin back onto the table.

Kurt's face turned five shades of red. Mine probably matched his. Advaith and Matt nudged him, laughing. I tried not to look at him, hoping not to make it worse. He finally walked over to the bar with his friends. When Hope excused herself to go to the restroom, my eyes flickered to Jenner's. His fingers deftly pulled the napkin with Kurt's message written on it, toward him. With his eyes still on mine, he crumpled up the napkin into his fist. Then he shoved it into a long neck beer bottle on the table.

"I don't know what that means. Is that a jealousy thing? Is that an 'I don't want you talking to him' thing? Everything you do contradicts what you say."

It seemed every day we took one step forward and two steps back. I couldn't keep up with him. With his moods.

"You look adorable," he said softly.

"Adorable?" I repeated.

"Well, Judge," Hope said playfully as she plopped up next to him. "You already said you don't text. I'm wondering your thoughts on walking me back to the hotel."

Jenner sloshed around what little liquid was left his in tumbler and said something quietly to just her. I couldn't make it out, but she smiled at me. An uneasy feeling rooted in the pit of my stomach.

They both stood. No way. He wasn't going with her. He wouldn't do that. But then he looked at me and shook his head. Shook his head? What did that mean? My heart accelerated. Kurt came back to the table and whispered in my ear.

"Sorry about that."

I acknowledged his words with a nod, not making it a big deal. I couldn't drag my eyes away from Jenner. I was completely over stimulated not knowing which way to turn or who to pay attention to.

Hope leaned into my other ear. "I think if you didn't work for him, he'd be fucking you tonight."

I giggled uncomfortably, wondering why she said that. The only person I wanted near my ears was going to walk out with my friend. Bethany tapped my hand.

"I think I may leave too. I'm sorry. We've been here longer than you and I've had enough."

"I get it. Totally ok. I'll walk out with you. I'm exhausted anyway."

By the time I turned back around, Hope and Jenner were gone. Panicked, I texted him.

Please don't...

That was all I sent. Bethany and I waited for her tab because Kurt had bought every drink of mine. As she got her credit card out, I turned to him.

"I'm sorry about that. I think I was so stunned that I didn't think to pick the napkin up. I really am sorry."

He shook his head. "Don't worry about it. I shouldn't have written that anyway. I stand by it, but I shouldn't have written it." His shy smile made me feel better.

"I just don't want to mix any sort of business with pleasure, ok?"

Sliding his sport coat on, he wrapped an arm around me. "If I hadn't drank so much, I never would have had the courage to write it. I agree with what you're saying."

We stepped out the door to find Jenner and Hope sitting on a bench just outside the pub. They both glanced at us, Kurt's arm still over my shoulders. Jenner's eyebrows rose, but I didn't acknowledge him. Advaith and Matt walked ahead of Bethany, Kurt and me. And as we got closer to the hotel, I glanced back to see if either Hope or Jenner had followed. They hadn't.

Inside the hotel, I hugged Kurt.

"If I don't see you at the conference tomorrow, I'll see you in court," I laughed, feeling the full effect of the martinis in my head. "Bye guys," I said to Advaith and Matt.

Bethany and I rode the elevator up. She got off on the seventh floor. I rode up to the sixteenth, staring at the blank screen beneath the text I'd sent to him. He hadn't responded. I prayed for bubbles to appear, but nothing. I closed my eyes until the elevator dinged.

After undressing in my room, I slid Jenner's t-shirt from last night over my head. The fabric had absorbed his masculine, torturous smell. I allowed a few tears to fall. For just a second, I would give into my sorrow. Tears for Pops and tears for Jenner. I didn't cry often, but sometimes a good release was necessary. My phone dinged, shaking me out of my melancholy, and I rushed to read the text. Dr. Shu. Not the man I wanted to hear from.

Lucy. Your grandfather is doing better. I would like to speak with you when you have time tomorrow. Let me know what works for you.

I texted back right away.

I can call you now. Is something wrong?

Don't be silly. I'd have called you if something were wrong. I'd like to converse about his current care and other options.

Something inside of me cracked as the damn burst. Couldn't I catch a break? The moment I'd dreaded for the past couple of years was crashing in on me. A full care facility in the city. I liked the place closer to the farm. Our roles had reversed—I had been the caretaker of my caretaker. And with my career and with Hank's age, I always knew we were on borrowed time. I just thought it would be longer. I lay on the bed trying to decide what to text back as tears spilled onto the cotton sheets.

The knock at the door startled me. I was so wrapped up in my thoughts about Pops that for a few minutes, I'd actually forgotten about Jenner. I peeked out the peephole. Jenner rested against the doorframe with his head down. For a short second, I contemplated not opening the door. I didn't need this right now. But before I could change my mind, the door was open.

"You're crying."

It wasn't a question, more of a statement. I tried to close the door, but he stopped it with his foot.

"Tell me," he instructed. "Why are you crying?"

Sometimes, he could be completely emotionless. I looked at the clock, trying to determine if it was feasible for him to have bedded Hope.

"Were you with her?"

"Is that why you're upset? Because of Hope?" His voice rose in shock.

Defeated and well aware that he hadn't answered my question, I handed him my phone, showing him the conversation with Dr. Shu. At the same time, his phone rang, and he turned away to answer it. My thoughts flashed back to that night not so long ago when we had once before been interrupted by his phone.

"What's up?" he answered.

"Yes. I'm with her now." He paused as his drunken eyes bore into me. "Thank you."

"Are the tears because of your grandfather?"

I tossed my phone onto the bed. "Who was that?"

"Dr. Shu. He thought you might be upset."

Jenner seemed to cover all his bases well. "I know that we aren't supposed to…I mean that it's unethical and well, you can with Hope, and I didn't know if…"

All I wanted to hear was that he wanted me, but something inside of me knew those words wouldn't come. His career meant more to him.

And, that was ok. Mine did too. I think. Why would he risk everything for a woman he barely knew? His father was a freaking Supreme Court Justice…the most powerful judge in the United States. My father was in prison.

I never really finished my statement. His alcohol-induced gaze took in all of me from head to toe. And as if dismissing a thought, he shook his head and took two deliberate steps toward me. His hands raked over my skin, through my hair until his fingers wrapped around my neck and pulled me into him. I kept my eyes open until our lips met.

Chapter 13

Objection

Jenner

Christ, the taste of her mouth. I wondered if she remembered the taste of mine like I remembered hers. I'd never wanted a woman as much as I wanted Lucy in that second. When she walked into the bar earlier wearing those skimpy Nike shorts and that Cubs t-shirt, she looked absolutely gorgeous. But seeing her in my t-shirt was literally my undoing.

As my tongue slid into the warmth of her delicious mouth, her tongue softly touched mine, and then retreated. No. More. More. I needed more. Alcohol swam through my veins, leading to a harsher kiss. I pressed my lips insistently to hers, and it wasn't until she whimpered that my eyes shot open panicked that I'd hurt her. Her eyelids, still red from crying, were all I saw before I softened the kiss once again. With my finger, I lifted her chin so our mouths could meld more perfectly together. And, they did, effortlessly.

When her body relaxed into mine, I smiled, trying not to end the kiss. I had no idea what tomorrow would hold, but I was going to make the most of tonight and this precious time with Lucy.

"I don't know where to go from here, Jenner," she whispered, our lips still touching.

"You don't have to know. I've got you."

My eyes never ventured from hers as I unfastened my belt, unbuttoned my slacks and allowed them to drop to the floor. She methodically undid each button on my shirt, exposing another one of my white t-shirts. Tugging behind my neck, I pulled the shirt off. She could have this one too.

Her touch literally took my breath as her fingertips outlined my pecs dragging down and across the length of my abs.

"Jenner." Her voice was barely audible. "I need you."

Her pleading tone tugged at my heart. There was no way in hell I was going to deny her. Not tonight. With both hands, I grabbed the hem of the white shirt she wore, and her arms shot upward, urging me on. She was braless, and her breasts were beautiful. My mind played back our first night together, and she seemed more beautiful in this moment.

Her warm hand cupped the bulge in my boxer briefs as her forehead rested on my chest. I kissed the top of her hair, enjoying her gentle touch. Then I caressed her breasts smiling at her slight gasp.

"Lay down," I directed softly, remembering her words from months ago of wanting to be told what to do. I wanted to be everything she wanted.

Once her calves hit the mattress, she sat on the bed and scooted back, her typically bright eyes going dark—heavy with desire.

"Don't move," I whispered, leaning in and snagging her panties with my fingertips, then slowly inching them down her legs. Once her panties were off, she closed her legs, resting her knees together.

I shook my head. "No way. Over ruled, counselor," I said in a low voice, pulling her ankle toward me and exposing her wetness.

I hadn't gone down on a woman in several years. To me, that was more intimate than sex. Fucking someone was easy and protected. Going down on someone was vulnerable and raw.

With her ankle in my hand, I dropped kisses between her foot and her knee, then continued up her luscious thigh as her eyes followed the fiery path my lips scorched. When I dropped a final kiss on her protruding pelvic bone, I wondered for a second when she last ate. I knew her mind was in a hundred different places. But for tonight, I would have her full attention.

As my lips inched closer to her wetness, her legs shook in anticipation. The moment I tasted her for the first time, her entire body became putty in my hands.

It took hardly any time for her hips to arch to me, her fists to tangle into my hair and her body to release itself due to my touch. The slight whimpers that echoed up her throat slayed me. Jesus. As hard as I fought it, my heart fell into her possession.

Resting my body on top of hers, I glanced down at her hooded eyes, which gazed up at me longingly.

"Jenner," she whispered.

A swallow got wedged in my throat at her silent plea. I didn't know what she wanted, but I knew that whatever it was…it was hers. As I slowly slid my unprotected cock inside of her, I realized my heart was as unguarded and vulnerable as my cock, and I wasn't sure which was worse. But I sure as hell didn't stop.

The dawn light crept through the cracked opening of the curtains.

Lucy's breaths were slow, steady, and deep. There was a slight part to her pouty lips. I could still taste her on mine. It never felt more right than waking up with her next to me. With the utmost stillness, I snuck from beneath the covers—the cold air caused a shiver.

After I got dressed, I headed down to the concierge lounge to grab her coffee. The smell of sweet baked goods blasted me as I entered. Man, I was starving. Trying to juggle two cups of coffee and a couple of sweet rolls, I carefully turned around and came face to face with Daryanne Watkins.

"Judge," she spat out hatefully.

"Ms. Watkins." I attempted to step around her, but she moved the same direction I did blocking me.

"Don't Ms. Watkins me, Jenner," she hissed. "Your dick has been inside me. I'd have more respect for you if you simply said, fuck off."

I nodded, refusing eye contact. I'd lived with her harmless threats for two years. "Ok, Daryanne, fuck off."

Within a split second, her angry face was within inches of mine. Eye contact at this point was unavoidable. "Don't you forget, I could destroy you."

"No you can't, Daryanne. I fucked you before you became the first assistant to the DA."

"Oh please. We both know that if that sordid little detail got out, your daddy would be sooo disappointed and decisions regarding your cases would be scrutinized." Her well-manicured eyebrows shot up.

"I still have the notarized letter—proof that I ended our relationship the moment you were hired. Get over it. It's been two years." This time, I stepped past her.

"Speaking of two, Judge Weber. You're in a hotel, it's 6:45 in the morning and you are scooping up two coffees and two cinnamon rolls. What's her name?"

My irate eyes slammed into her, hoping to mask the strained expression I felt. I was fully aware of our audience of a select few. "Like I already said, fuck off, Daryanne."

CHAPTER 14

APPEALED

Lucy

Jenner and I hadn't talked much since I woke up to a hot cup of coffee and a cinnamon roll. His note was simple. *Thank you. I enjoy every moment with you. J*

I assumed we were back to not talking. Honestly, I couldn't keep up anymore.

While the conference had been great, work hadn't stopped while I was gone, so it had piled up on my desk. Cases that needed filed, cases that needed revoked, cases that needed reviewed. Motions. Briefs. More often than not, I spent my days overwhelmed. Every single child mattered to me. I remembered my Mimi telling me once that if all the fish in the ocean washed ashore, I should do everything I could to get them back into the water but know that there was no way to save them all. I knew that. But I was damn sure going to try.

A week had passed since our night at the hotel. I hadn't seen Jenner at work, and he hadn't texted. In theory, neither had I. But, as far as I was concerned, the ball was in his court. Walking up the three flights of stairs to my apartment was the extent of exercise I was getting these days. The moment I stepped into the hallway, the sweet smell of Midge's handiwork was in the air, bringing with it a smile that spread from cheek to cheek.

The undeniable smell of vanilla wafted up my nose as I slid the key into the deadbolt. Midge was the only person who had a key to my apartment. Tears nipped at my eyes when I spotted the pot simmering on the stove and what looked like glazed vanilla scones on a platter. God, I love that woman.

The night came and went without a word from Jenner…again. I tried to brace myself for the growing hurt in my chest. I wasn't typically a skeptic—but with regards to Jenner—I was either a cynic or a realist. Maybe both. It was what it was. I'd be forever indebted to him for his help with Pops.

The following morning at work, one of the legal interns met me with paperwork from Chicago Police Department. After reading over the police report about a six year old girl who'd been sexually abused from her nineteen-year-old stepbrother, I darted straight to my office to start the Ex Parte paperwork. This wasn't on my list of things to do—but took priority over everything. That was the thing about child in need of care work…certain cases took precedence.

As I entered the information into the system, my personal phone buzzed. I glanced at the lit screen, glanced back at my computer, then quickly back to the phone. Jenner!

My heart revved as I resisted the impulse to scream in elation. I unlocked my phone and touched the screen to open the text. My smile quickly faded.

Stop what you're doing and come to my office.

Cautiously, I glanced around. No one saw me looking at my phone. There was no reason not to get up and go, yet I stayed glued to my seat. Frozen. His text gave no hint. Was it good? Was it bad? There was no way in hell he'd do a single sexual thing in that entire building…so office sex wasn't optional.

Surely this wasn't about Pops. My desk phone rang and the caller ID read Judge Weber. Suddenly, I felt sick. With shaky hands, I picked up the receiver. The courthouse was across the street.

"What's wrong?" I whispered.

"I need you to stand up, leave your office and come straight to mine.

Am I clear?"

"Judge, please. Tell me what's wrong."

"Lucy. Do as I said, ok?"

He said Lucy. Not Ms. Edwards. This was personal. I didn't wait for another word. I hung up the phone, slid on my jacket, grabbed a random folder off my desk and casually left my office. At the elevator, I poked the button, trying to maintain composure but on the inside, I was coming apart. This was serious. Someone knew something. We were in trouble. That had to be it.

Once inside the courthouse, I rode another elevator to his floor. The elevator moved slower than I'd ever recalled, and as I stepped off, Deb, the guardian ad litem was there wiping her tears.

"You ok?" I honestly didn't want to get distracted, but I couldn't not ask.

She shook her head. "Yes. It just makes me sad. I wish I would have listened to you."

"Listened to me? What are you talking about it?"

"You don't know?"

I shrugged.

"Paige Engle was killed."

Engle. Engle. Engle. My mind ran through my cases, then recognition settled in. My knees buckled, and thankfully, the wall was close. She'd killed her. Her mother had killed her.

"Ms. Edwards?" Jenner's voice jarred me. Both Deb and I watched him walk slowly in our direction. His strained expression focused on me. The composure I fought to maintain just minutes before faded as my face crumbled.

"How?" I whispered.

"I've got this, Ms. Scheels," Jenner said coldly.

Deb hugged me. "I'm sorry, Lucy."

Over her shoulder and through blurred eyes, I could only focus on Jenner. I didn't want to cry in front of him. My splotchy face and red nose were inevitable, however. His disheveled appearance surprised me. It looked as if he had run his hands through his hair a hundred times. His tie was loose.

Deb stepped on the elevator, leaving us alone in the hallway. I pushed away from the wall and moved toward him.

"How did it happen?"

He shook his head, raking his fingers through his hair again. His shoulders slumped. "I went to the emergency room last night when I got the call. Mother brought her in unconscious." His tired eyes darted up to mine. "They're doing an autopsy."

When his voice cracked, I felt my chin tremble. Then suddenly, he wrapped me in a hug.

"Jesus, Lucy."

Every bit of his professional façade and mine was thrown to the wind with the emotion we felt. I fell apart in his arms as his tight embrace apologized a thousand times over.

Somewhere in my mind, I heard the ding, but it wasn't until Jenner's body stiffened and his arms fell to his side that I noticed a tall, blonde standing behind me. The woman from the bar. My boss, Hope had said. Perfect, what a great first impression.

"Judge Weber. I heard you lost one," she commented with snootiness to her tone.

"Ms. Watkins, this is Lucy Edwards. She's the ADA on the case."

With her fingertip, she touched my nose. "Oh. Poor girl. I don't think we've met. Daryanne Watkins. I'm the Chief ADA. And I'm not sure if you're aware, but ethically, hugging the judge is a big no-no."

"Daryanne. Enough. She was upset about the child." Jenner turned to me. "Ms. Edwards, please go to my office. I'll be there shortly."

This woman was my boss? I blotted my tears with my sleeve.

"Ms. Watkins," I cleared my throat and spoke. "I recommended that this child remain in out of home placement."

"That's correct," Jenner added. "It was my decision to return the girl home."

The woman swatted her hand his way not even giving me a look. "Please, you have judicial immunity. We will somehow get this blamed on the supervising agency. Besides, all judges have a dead baby on their caseloads."

"What?" I asked.

"Ms. Edwards. Go to my office," Jenner demanded.

Angry, frustrated, sad...I spun around and headed toward Jenner's office.

When I rounded the corner, I heard her ask, "Hugging her in the hallway, Jenner? That means fucking her behind closed doors."

Immediately, I stopped walking.

"I'm not doing this with you, Daryanne. But, no, I'm not fucking her, and honestly, green doesn't suit you."

"Fuck off, Jenner. If you are fucking her, she's as good as fired."

My jaw fell slack. Who the hell was this woman?

"Fire away. Nothing you do will get me back in your bed."

Fire away? It was as if a steel knife sliced my windpipe, blocking air from going either way. The wall stabilized me once again until he hustled around the corner, nearly careening into me. His beautiful jawline hardened.

"Ms. Edwards. Please go to my office like I've asked."

For the first time since I'd gotten his text, I was reminded of where we were. Nothing should take precedence over that. That was of the utmost importance. My heart longed for first place, but it would have to settle for second. And my mind, it couldn't keep up with any of this.

The sad, confused fog wasn't broken by Jenner's presence. When he opened the doors to his division, his assistant thankfully, wasn't there. I sighed.

"Come on," he said, breezing past me into his office. He stopped at the door, waiting for me to comply, then rested his hand at the small of my back before he closed the door behind us.

"You will have no legal responsibility with regards to the respondent, Lucy."

"Her name is Paige. Was Paige." Tears brimmed my eyes as I sat. "And it sounds like you won't either." I hoped the terseness in my tone was evident.

He released a pent-up breath, clawing at his hair, then collapsed in a chair opposite me. "I'm sorry for what happened to her, Lucy," he whispered; his eyes burrowed into my soul.

"That *respondent*," I hissed throwing up air quotes. "Was a little girl who depended on me. On you. On us to keep her safe. We failed her, Jenner." I shot up out of my chair as the tears spilled over.

"Look. I know you're upset, Lucy. I get it. But I have to follow the law. I don't know how many times I have to say that to you." Jenner sat against his desk, crossing his feet at the ankles.

"The law protects the parents not the children. You had a child to protect. To keep out of the hands of her mother. You failed."

I wanted to hurt him with my words.

"Lucy. If I'd have sided with you, I would have been appealed."

"So. The fuck. What!" I raised my voice, and he shot upright glaring at me. "Maybe the child wouldn't have been killed while being appealed!"

CHAPTER 15

JUDICIAL INDISCRETIONS

Jenner

"Ms. Edwards," I cautioned through gritted teeth. This was exactly why what we were doing was wrong.

She lifted her chin even as tears made little paths down her cheeks. Damn this girl had spunk and sass like I'd never known. "Maybe you'd have gotten appealed, maybe you wouldn't have. At least your defense would be that you aired on the side of the child. Maybe she'd be moving in with her grandparents right now rather than in a morgue. We'll never know."

Fuck, I was caught somewhere between wanting to admonish her, wanting to comfort her and wanting to bend her over my desk. I reminded myself where we were.

"It's professional, Lucy. Not personal. My decision was based on the law, like I've said several times. You know…the law. The class you apparently skipped in law school." I blurted the words out unthinkingly.

The flare of her nostrils almost made me smile, but when her fists clenched, I flinched. "How about you fucking the Deputy District Attorney? Was that professional or personal? Somehow that fit into your version of the law?"

I had no idea what she had heard between Daryanne and me, but clearly it was enough. She seemed unnecessarily jealous. This shit could not go down here.

"I can't do this here, Lucy. I…I can't protect you here. We are too exposed. Come to my house tonight. We can talk about it then."

"Come to your house? What did you not understand about what my boss just said to you? She will fire me, Jenner."

Undoubtedly, Daryanne would pitch a fit if she found out that I was… whatever it was I was doing with Lucy. I had to find a way to keep this hidden. All along I'd been hesitant. Resistant. And for good reason. But hearing those words come out of Lucy's mouth devastated me. I wasn't ready to give her up.

"Please come," I asked as she fidgeted close to my door. She was going to bail, I could feel it.

"Why, Jenner? So you can fuck me again, knowing that we will never be more?"

Jesus. I wanted to tell her I wanted it all with her, but I fell short of saying the words.

"No, Lucy. I…"

"And seriously?" she interrupted. "Have you been in a relationship with her the entire time? Are you two even over?"

I took two measured steps toward her shaking my head.

Her chin trembled. "Is that why you said we could never be more? Because you were fucking her?"

I'd never known her to run away from a fight. But damn, I swear she was inching closer and closer to the door.

"Lucy."

"Jenner. She is everything I'm not. And nothing I want to be. I don't understand. If you ever picked her, I have no idea what you'd ever want with me."

"Please come over and let me explain."

"Has she been to your house?"

"Fuck, no."

Her features softened, and I stole the opportunity to dart toward her. I cupped her cheeks in my palms. "No woman has been to my home, Lucy. You fail to understand, and I don't know how to make you understand. This is the only way I know."

She looked confused at first, then I kissed her persuasively, needing her to understand that I wanted to make her happy. Initially, she resisted, trying to shake her head, but then my tongue invaded her mouth. Finally, when she conceded to the kiss, her tongue slowly mingled with mine and she moaned. I lifted her beneath her arms and carried her to my desk. What the fuck was I doing?

I shoved a file to the floor, sat her on the desk my father had bought me and wedged myself between her legs. It only took me seconds to skim beneath her skirt, flick my finger beneath her panties and find her wet. When she spread her legs even further apart, my cock pressed against the seam of my slacks.

With one finger buried inside of her, my thumb found her sweet spot and set that pace that I'd used on her before. Once again, I covered her mouth with mine, breathing unspoken apologies and growing regret. Pleasing her was my job today. And though I was neglecting my real job, I needed this as much as she did. Her heart was hurting, her mind was jacked up…all because of me. This was the least I could do. Her fingers suddenly clawed at my dress shirt as her ragged breaths breezed past her lips. My eyes scanned over every inch of her face as she came apart by the pleasure of my hand.

I swallowed hard as I memorized her expression. I wanted to see that look on her face every day. I thirsted for what she had to offer me. Yet, once the pleasure began to fade, she readjusted her panties, her skirt, and stood, blood invading her cheeks.

"Jenner," she whispered. "What have we done?"

"Don't say anything, Lucy. For just a second, I wanted you to feel good. That's all."

Her eyes bulged. "I can't take care of you right now and…" Frazzled, she picked up the file I'd sent to the floor earlier.

"I'm not asking you to. I needed to take care of you. To show you…"

"I have to go. I have to get back to work. I have cases to file and…oh dear God, what if I get fired?"

I don't even think she was talking to me.

"Please come over later." After jotting down my address, I handed her the paper.

She stared at me. The mascara below her eyes smudged beautifully.

I wanted her to stay in my office, but an uncomfortable silence had fallen between us. As she spun around and walked out—a piece of me wondered if that was the last time I'd ever touch her.

CHAPTER 16

UNDER OATH

Lucy

Henley looked gorgeous as usual when she sat next to me at Tony's Tavern. Tony's had served as our meeting place through law school; I just never had a drink in front of me like I did tonight. And it wasn't my first. Vodka now swam through my veins rather than hurt and confusion.

"What's up? You look like shit," she said with a smile, tossing popcorn in her mouth. A Tony's Tavern bonus—a free popcorn machine that was always full for poor college students.

"Thank you. I need your help," I admitted, shaking my head. "Your advice."

"Of course." She motioned to the bartender who already knew her drink.

"Henley. This is so so so confidential. Like so so so so." Hopefully she understood this with the multiple so's.

She took off her jacket and hung it on the hook outside the booth. Her eyes filled with concern.

"OK. Are you in trouble?"

The waitress slid Henley's red beer toward her. I waited to talk until the waitress was gone.

"Remember the guy from the club. The farmers market guy that met me at the hotel?"

"The cherry popper?" she smiled, eating more popcorn.

I nodded. "Is that really what kids are saying these days, Henley?"
She grinned. "But, yes. That's the one."

"How could I forget? That guy was sexy as hell."

"Yes. Well, I've seen him on and off, I guess you could say, for a couple of months."

Her eyes shot wide. "You've been keeping it a secret, you big ho!"

I grinned, but the happiness never reached my eyes.

"That's not all, obviously. What's wrong? Tell me the rest," she said.

The vodka seemed strong as I downed my drink. I needed it strong to get through this conversation. After clearing my throat, I looked her dead in the eye.

"He is the Honorable Jenner Weber."

She shrugged. "A judge? So…"

"So…think United States Supreme Court Justice Weber."

"Wow, the Supreme's son? Nice but so?"

Here came the biggest punch line of my joke of a life.

"He's the child in need of care judge. My judge."

Her hand clasped over her mouth as she froze with a wide-eyed stare.
My best friend's reaction said it all.

I kept silent as I allowed my words to soak in.

"Lu-cy." My name sounded like two separate words coming out of her mouth. "Your judge? As in he presides over the cases you prosecute?"

Disapproval lurked in her question.

I nodded slowly—knowing her brain was firing on all synapses.

"OK. OK. It's ok. You haven't fucked him since you found out he was the judge, right?"

My telling stare was all she needed to answer her own question.

"Jesus Christ, Lucy!"

"Does him getting me off on his desk count?"

Both her hands shot up covering her face. "Is that what they mean by 'being guided by the standards of professional conduct?" The rest of her beer was gone in about three gulps. "This job was your dream job. You are doing exactly what you went to school for. What are you doing? This could ruin everything."

"I think I'm in love with him."

She did the staring this time. "What do you think the New York Commission on Judicial Discipline might think of that?"

"Henley, please. I really need a friend."

After motioning for another drink, she turned her full attention to me. "I am a friend. A fucking great friend who is telling you to stop."

Closing my eyes, I rested my head against the back of the booth.

"What do you want me to say, Luce? That it's ok? What the hell is *he* saying?"

"He seems as crazy as Kanye some days. Hot and cold. Up and down."

"In and out—of you, obviously." A slight smile touched her lips. "Seriously. He's fine with it?"

I shook my head. "No. He knows it's not ok. He's said it can't happen. He's talked about the consequences. I don't know. Somehow something still happens."

We sat in silence for what seemed like the longest few minutes.

"What do you want from me? Are you just telling me or are you looking for advice?"

"That's not all…"

"Oh, fuck me. Tell me you're not pregnant with some judicial spawn. Or tell me Daddy Justice didn't find out."

I wanted to tell her about the Munchausen case but honestly, that played second fiddle to the rest of this.

"Apparently, he had a previous relationship with the Deputy DA in my office." With just those words, she folded her arms on top of the table and rested her forehead on her arms. So, I didn't stop there. "She saw us together. She said she would fire me if she found out that I was in his bed. Well, she didn't tell me, but she said that to him."

"Well for God's sake, Lucy. What are you questioning?"

I rubbed my temples. When I said it out loud to her, my choice seemed obvious. But leaving Jenner was not as easy as she made it sound. "I don't know."

"Seriously, is this guy worth losing your career?"

My eyes were drawn to the front door of the Tavern. Jenner had magically appeared in the doorway. I'd never seen him look so disheveled. Droopy sweats, a West Point sweatshirt and a baseball cap completed his attire. His desperate eyes locked in on mine. What the hell? Was he following me?

JENNER

Stopping at Judge Eichman's house wasn't on my agenda, but desperation led me to his driveway. I sat tapping my thumb on the steering wheel staring up at the bright porch light. Larry had been a friend of my father's and a mentor to me. Though he was our administrative judge, I trusted our friendship went deeper than that. But what I was about to do could never be undone.

The dongs of the doorbell resonated through the big, wooden door. Then I heard Cindy announce she was coming from inside. Age had gotten the better of her, but she still lit up the room with her smile.

"Jenner!" she said with a happy smile. "What brings you here?"

I leaned in brushing a kiss over her cheek.

"Hello, Cindy. So good to see you. Is Larry around?"

Stepping inside, she closed the door behind me and motioned me down the hallway. "He's super busy. Watching Survivor, I think."

I chuckled.

"Larry, Jenner is here," she announced, rounding the corner.

"Ah, Jenner. Please sit down. And be quiet. We are at tribal counsel."

I shook my head laughing as Cindy rolled her eyes and left us alone. Then I sat and listened quietly as Jeff Probst talked to the tribe. I used to love this show, but somewhere along the lines, I stopped watching. It wasn't long before the votes were read, someone was voted out and their torch was snubbed. Then, the TV was off.

"What the hell is wrong?" he asked.

I glanced up at him as my index finger rubbed repeatedly at a hangnail on my thumb.

"What makes you think something is wrong?"

"What is it, Jenner? Are you in trouble?"

"Maybe."

Larry got up from his recliner and walked over to a liquor stand where he poured both of us a drink. Once he handed me the glass tumbler, I smelled it before I sipped. Scotch. Not a fan. But I hit it.

"Am I judge or friend for this scenario?"

"Friend. Sort of. Fuck, I don't know. It's career related."

"OK." He sat in a different chair. "You gonna tell me or not?"

"I'm in love with a prosecutor. And not just any prosecutor. She's the one assigned to my division. Remember when you told me to end it with Daryanne? And I did. Straight away. Zero regrets. Well, Daryanne saw me hugging this girl and now she is out for blood. I tried to tell Daryanne that there was nothing. I don't think she bought it. She threatened to fire the girl."

I watched Larry lace his fingers behind his head.

"And you've been fucking this girl while you've presided over her cases?"

"I have."

"Though the ethics board won't give a shit what you say, have you shown her bias?"

"I have not." That was truth.

He scratched through his over-grown beard. "Does Daryanne have any evidence?"

"No. Just speculation with what she saw."

"Then don't give her any."

I knew what he meant by that...dump Lucy. I tried to wrap my mind around not having Lucy in my life.

"I'm not sure I can do that. Is there any chance of reassignment? Get me out of the child in need of care division?"

He blew out a breath, staring at the blank television screen. "Jenner. You're young to even be a district court judge. You know that. I can't move you to criminal or civil at this point. Domestic possibly, but I'd have to speak to the other judges."

"I'm sure you'll be met with resistance. No one wants CINC." Lucy did. She wanted to save every damn child out there. "What about reassigning her? Maybe a formal request to the DA to put her in domestic?" This would kill her.

"And why is it you can't just leave her alone?"

Finishing the scotch, I shrugged. "God damn, I've tried. I've seriously tried."

"Tried as in past tense? As in you are done trying?" Concern boiled in his tone and his eyes.

"Yes. I believe I am done trying."

Larry shot to his feet. "The hell you are. If I have to call your father, I will," he threatened. "You end this. You end this now. You end it for your career and you end it for hers. Because of who you are, you'll work again. She won't. You know it and I know it."

Hearing his words was like a searing brand on my chest.

"I'm serious, Jenner. Grow some balls and tell this girl it's over. This thing has the potential to destroy more than just you. Your father included. Take care of this before it takes care of you."

Stunned, my brain slowly absorbed the words, not fully believing them. My mind declared war on what he said, attempting to refute him. To negate what he said. Then my brain started looking at it from his side. Just because she made me happy didn't mean we were meant to be, I rationalized. Three days passed since I'd asked her to come to my house. She hadn't come. Maybe she'd already let it go. Maybe I was hanging onto something that wasn't even a thing.

When I got to my car my phone buzzed. Before I pulled it from my pocket, I knew it was her—I just had a feeling and relief settled through me. I started the car, looked at my screen and was surprised to see my friend Mitchell's name. I opened the text and a picture popped up. Lucy and her friend from the club. Mitchell texted just below it: Hey, look, there's Miss Hey you guys, I'm tired and gonna head out.

I shook my head. They knew me well enough to know I didn't go home with girls, and I certainly hadn't told them that night where I was going. Clearly, they'd figured it out and watched me talk to her.

I shot a text back. *Fuck off.*

When I saw the little bubble—I waited for his words. *She's crying at Tony's. You break another heart?*

Lucy was crying. I didn't respond to Mitchell. I simply put the car in drive and drove. Like a mad man.

Tony's Tavern had been a go-to for law students for years. Not sure why, but Lucy didn't strike me as a regular. My hope was to walk in, go have a seat with the guys, and monitor her reaction. But when I opened the door and spotted her sad, green eyes, my entire planet cracked. Larry's warning flew out of my mind, my prick of a father fleeted away, my young career took a back seat—I'd become obsessed about making her life better, chasing away her pain, about loving her completely.

"Jenner!" one of the guys shouted, and my eyes abandoned hers to see them pointing at me. Their laughing eyes jotted back and forth between Lucy and me. Aggravated, I navigated my way over to them.

"Look at who hustled down to the bar after only one text," Jeff chuckled.

"You look like shit, man." Brian threw out.

I readjusted my ball cap—I had forgotten I still had it on—and wondered if Lucy's eyes were still on me?

"Shut the fuck up," I said, sitting where Lucy would be in my peripheral. "Why the hell are you guys even here?"

Brian pointed at the TV in the corner. A baseball game was on. The one sport I hated.

"And what, you thought coming here you'd find some young, pretty law students to watch with?"

"Yep. That redhead especially," Mitchell laughed.

A cross between a smirk and a sneer crossed my face.

"Can I get you a drink?" a waitress asked, calming my irritation…a little.

"I'll have a bourbon and water."

Jeff grabbed the waitress's arm. "Would you get that redhead over there a drink on me?"

"No, she won't," I said with a serious face. The waitress eyeballed me, and I shook my head.

Jeff's smile widened, and he motioned for the waitress to go on, then he kicked my chair. I glanced at the TV.

"So, you still seeing her?"

"It's complicated, but what difference does it make?

Brian chimed in. "For starters she and her friend are hot as fuck."

"Well then, buy her friend a drink."

All three of my friends chuckled. "The great Jenner Weber is whipped."

They had no clue. Hell, I didn't have a clue.

"Excuse me, Judge?"

Hearing judge always made me nervous. Lucy's friend was standing in front of me. Angry?

"Yes?" I glanced back toward the table and Lucy was gone.

She leaned down. "Leave. Her. Alone." She whispered roughly into my ear. "This is going to be harder for her since she gave her virginity to you. But her career means everything to her so please walk away."

My mouth fell open as she leaned back, and her eyes held a warning of their own.

"Virginity?"

The girl's brows pulled together as she pulled on the strings of her sweatshirt. "She didn't tell you?"

I swallowed dryly, shaking my head.

"Please, let her go," she said as she walked away.

Stunned, I wasn't sure what to do. I stood, then paced, then stood still again, staring at the door she must have gone through earlier. The guys said something I didn't comprehend as my fists clenched and unclenched. I made some lame excuse to the guys and bolted outside, trying to capture my breath. Lucy was a virgin? That night at the hotel—I thought back to how I had flipped her over and pounded into her. Jesus. The way she sucked me…like she was nervous, timid, unsure. Had she never done that before either? My mind raced with questions. And I wanted fucking answers.

CHAPTER 17

PROBABLE CAUSE

Lucy

The line in the restroom was ridiculous, and I put lip gloss on before I walked out. My heart sunk—Jenner was gone. I'd told Henley to go on since she needed to get out of there. But I held out hope that Jenner might come over and talk to me. At the very least, stay. It had been difficult to keep my eyes off of him as he sat there with his friends. Of course, once again showing up out of the blue where I was.

I flung my purse over my shoulder, cast a glance at his ogling friends and headed out. I must have read his eyes wrong when he first came in. For a second, it felt like he wanted me or maybe something from me. I don't know. Henley was right. I had to try to save my career and move on.

The cold air knocked me in the face when I opened the door. It was brutal. Winter was breathing down our necks, ready or not. I adjusted my scarf just a bit tighter. When I spun away from the wind, Jenner stood there. Damn that ball cap.

"You were a virgin?"

I swallowed. "No," I spat out like it was the stupidest question ever. How the hell did he find out?

"Lucy. Why didn't you tell me?"

"Tell you what, Jenner?" I acted disgusted by his accurate accusation. I tried to step past him. "Taxi." I held up my hand hailing a cab.

He clutched my upper arm spinning me around. "I'll take you home."

"Stop. I got here by myself. I can get home by myself."

"I'm taking you home, Lucy. We need to talk. Plus, it's ridiculously cold."

I wasn't sure how much longer I could keep up my resolve. "Jenner, I can't," I whispered.

"This isn't open for discussion, Lucy. Get in my car."

Freezing, I conceded and got in. The car was strangely quiet. Neither of us spoke on the thirty-minute ride home. Not a peep. Henley had to have opened her freaking big mouth while I was in the restroom. My mind raced a thousand different directions trying to decide how I'd defend my decision to lose my v-card to a stranger. When we got inside the apartment, the cold quietness continued.

"Are you seriously going to ignore me? This discordance between us…"

"Discordance? No one says that shit, Jenner."

"Damn it, Lucy. Why the hell didn't you tell me you were a virgin?"

I threw my arms in the air. "What difference would it have made?" I yelled.

He collapsed onto the sofa and stared at me, something indescribable in his eyes. "Is that why you just threw sex out there that night? You were on a mission?"

I stood against the archway of the living room door. "So, what if I was? Yes. I went to the bar that night planning to lose my virginity. That sounds awful, I know. I just was tired of it being there."

"Why didn't you tell me?"

"Really, Jenner? I was like the last millennial virgin. What would I have said? Hey, I know I just picked you up in a bar, but would you mind robbing me of my virginity?"

His angry eyes bore into me. "I had a right to know."

"I didn't want you to know."

"Why me? Why did you choose me, Lucy?"

Inhaling the deepest of breaths, I whispered. "I don't think I did. I think you chose me."

We sat opposite each other, our eyes glued together. Everything that didn't make sense about me made sense when I was with him. I saw the best part of me in his eyes, and yet at the same time I was trying to remember my promise to Henley, I tried to stop what was happening.

"What's the big deal anyway?"

Jenner's knees cracked when he stood. And everything inside of me clenched as his slow, deliberate steps came in my direction.

"What's the big deal?" he repeated out loud. "The big deal, Lucy… is that I'm going to be your first. I'm going to be your only. And I'm going to be your last. That's how big of deal this is."

My lips parted as I exhaled. "Jenner…"

He grabbed the bill of his cap and turned it backward just as his mouth came down on mine. One. Two. Three. Four. Five soft pecks.

"Come on," he whispered, taking my hand and leading me to the bedroom.

"What are you doing?" I asked.

"I'm going to do this the way it should have been done that night."

I resisted.

"Please allow me this. Please let me show you that I would have respected the honor and the privilege. That I know how to do it without hurting you."

As we walked together into the bedroom, I searched for the courage I needed to tell him no. There was no way I would survive losing him again if we were together tonight. I already had so many memories that I'd never escape, and this would only add to it.

I resisted his tug on my hand. His eyes widened as he looked down at me.

"Jenner." I paused trying to find the words. "I can't."

His Adam's apple jutted out and back in. "Lucy. Please. I want to do this so differently."

I resisted the impulse to give in, but as I did, my throat tightened with regret. A few little hairs stuck out through the hole of his hat just above his forehead. Poised, professional and perfect.

I shook my head. "No."

The backs of his fingers brushed over my cheek. With eyes closed, I lowered my head away from his touch.

"Jenner. This is over. I feel awful because in the beginning you were so strong and you knew what was in our best interest. You knew."

"Fuck, being strong, Lucy."

"No!" I pushed away from him. "Listen to me. I didn't listen to you in the beginning. I pushed you and I'm sorry." My voice cracked. "You kept talking about ethics and responsibilities, and I get it now." Plump tears slowly navigated their way down my cheeks, and there wasn't a thing I could do about them.

"This isn't what you want, Lucy. I can smell you getting wet just standing here. You want me as much as I want you."

"It doesn't matter any more. I need this job, Jenner. What's between you and I will pass. We just have to leave it alone. You know it as well as I do."

His eyes rounded, and then the fire in them dimmed.

When he took a step back, that imaginary string attached between his body and my heart pulled taut. With every step he took away from me, it tugged a bit more. Awful anticipation of him leaving curled in my stomach as he lowered his head and turned for the door. Then anger tangled in with the other emotions roiling in my heart. This is what I said I wanted...I had no right to be angry.

His feet stopped moving and he turned back around, his eyes penetrating mine. Anger filled the void that he left. This wasn't fair. Nothing about this was fair.

"Lucy?"

"Jenner. Just go, ok?" I raised my voice.

"You're lying to yourself," he gritted.

He was going to dissect every word that came out of my mouth.

"Lying to myself?" I laughed. "Look. You went to Princeton. I went to a community college then City. Your dad is a supreme court judge. My father is a bank robber. Some of us are given jobs because of who we are. Some of us have to work at it. I can't afford to lose this job, Jenner. I can afford to lose you."

Following that, I braced myself for the wave of hurt that was coming. Jenner took off his ball cap, nodded once, put it back on with the bill to the front and walked out. The door closed with a click that jolted through my body.

It was only then, that I fell to my knees, my head reeling as my breaths came in sobbing gasps. Henley was right, I had to end it. Goodbye had always been inevitable. We'd danced around each other for months. Neither of us were sure if the risk was worth the price. I'd completely fallen in love with Jenner Weber and seeing him, smelling him, touching him only filled my head with doubt. Henley's pep talk made me believe I was strong enough to handle anything that came my way. I just wasn't sure if losing Jenner fell into that category. When I climbed onto my bed, I covered my entire body with the cold comforter. And I cried. His leaving had ripped the imaginary string right out of my chest, and my heart was gaping… now it was time to heal. I had to find a way to unlove him.

At work the next day, I still fought to recover my composure. I'd barely slept, and the hurt hadn't lessened.

"You ok?" Kurt asked as I handed him the copy of the paperwork he and I had discussed at the bar during the conference a month ago.

"Yes, why?" I lied. "There's the Order of Informal Supervision you asked for."

"Your face. Your eyes. They look…swollen? Lucy, what's wrong?"

I shook my head, trying to ward off the onslaught of tears that had only just stopped this morning. Thankfully no one was in the hallway except for Kurt, so when he put his arm around my shoulder, it didn't look totally inappropriate. I knew it was just a friendly gesture.

"Can I do anything?" he asked.

"No. But thank you."

"Can't we sign this OIS without going before the court?" he asked, and my hopes instantly rose. I didn't have the strength to go up against Jenner. Not today. Not in court. Not anywhere.

At the exact moment that his name passed through my mind, Jenner rounded the corner. Kurt's arm rested on my shoulder. Paranoid about the swelling in my face, I glanced down.

"Judge Weber," Kurt addressed.

"Hi, Judge," I whispered, unsure if he heard.

Jenner kept walking, only addressing us with a tight smile.

"Excuse me, Your Honor," Kurt hollered after Jenner, catching up to him. I took in long, measured breaths trying to soothe myself as I watched the two of them chat. Jenner shook his head never looking in my direction. When Kurt turned toward me, he shrugged, then shot his thumb toward the courtroom.

"He said no continuance."

Of course he did.

"You know," Kurt said before stepping through the courtroom doors, "I've always heard he was a dick, but after we all drank together, I thought he was pretty cool. He's kind of back to dick status for me."

Kurt's words made me smile momentarily as we made our way to our appropriate tables. His humor at least took the edge off if only for a few minutes. But, when the chamber doors came open and Jenner marched out in his robe, my heart plummeted. I kept my eyes on the paperwork.

"We are on the record in case number..." Jenner's voiced seemed softer than normal. My mind flashed to memories that I knew would haunt me forever—the first was the rush of his skin against mine. "Ms. Edwards?"

My eyes flew up to his. "Yes, Your Honor. I... uh...we are here on a motion to approve an order of informal supervision."

"I asked for appearances, Ms. Edwards. Is the Court distracting you from something more important?"

I wasn't sure if blood drained out of my face or if blood rushed to it...but the blast of heat was stifling. For a moment I thought I was going to pass out. I nodded. "I'm sorry, Judge. I thought that..."

"Ms. Edwards, please just state your appearance. This is not complicated." Jenner's jaw was tight and his eyes angry. The dick was back.

"Wow," Kurt added, shaking his head then Jenner's eyes shot to where Kurt sat.

"I'm sorry, Mr. Harris. When I want your opinion on how I run my courtroom, I'll give it to you. Appearance, Ms. Edwards?"

Feeling like a bobble head still nodding, I said, "May it please the court, Lucy Edwards appearing for the State."

My hands trembled, but nothing in comparison to my chin as I fought back tears. Fuck him, I thought to myself. Fuck him.

Chapter 18

Exclusive Jurisdiction

Jenner

The second glass of bourbon slid down my throat as smoothly as the first. That Kentucky hug was warm and tight clear down to my stomach. My feet rested on the coffee table, a motion from a case lay in my lap and a muted college basketball game played on the TV. I unbent a paperclip, poking the metal tip into my palm. Self-mutilation was never my thing, yet between the liquor and the pain from the metal—it didn't even begin to touch the regret over Lucy yesterday—self-harm was becoming an option.

When my doorbell rang, I tossed the half-empty bag of popcorn into the trash. The bag bounced off the side of the trash can, and popcorn and kernels fell across the stone floor. I tossed a napkin on the counter next to the empty pizza box and headed to the door. The porch was dark, so I flipped the light on and turned the knob.

"Fuck me. What do you want?"

My father, Mr. Supreme himself sauntered in. "This places smells appalling."

I shrugged as he stepped down into the living room.

"You're living like a pig. Is this because of this girl that I'm hearing about?"

Shit. "There's no girl."

His slicked back hair didn't budge as he bent down and picked up a throw pillow and tossed it back onto the sofa. Then, he leaned over and snagged the lidless bourbon bottle off the coffee table and drank straight from it. Unlike him, but I dug it.

"No female is worth detouring your career or ending it altogether."

"Detouring my career?" I laughed. Lucy would have laughed at those words too.

My father's hand came down hard on the granite stone in the kitchen. "Damn it, Jenner. What are you thinking? A young prosecutor?"

"You know, I wouldn't expect you to understand. We have something that requires emotion. Four months ago, when I met her, my world stopped spinning or maybe it started spinning," I laughed. "I don't know which. But I know when I'm with her, there is no place on earth I'd rather be." Fuck, my chest hurt.

"Your Hallmark card sentiment is unnecessary. I need you to focus. How do we end it with this Ms. Edwards."

A dry swallow got jammed in my throat. He'd been told her name. "It's already over," I quickly added.

"I swear to God, if this comes back on me because you can't keep your damn dick in your pants."

I shook my head. "Of course you're worried about you. It was never Mom and it was certainly never me. It's always been about you." No emotion was attached to my words.

"Jesus. You always have been the most ungrateful child. Ivy league education. Law school. Straight into a career so that you could get the judgeship. Were there more qualified candidates? Of course. But, I took care of you. And once again, all you have to say is what a terrible parent I was."

I rubbed my palms down the length of my face, wishing he'd go back to Washington. "Husband too," I added. "Don't forget. You were a terrible husband too."

There it was. That one vein that always popped out on his forehead when he got angry. A sense of satisfaction grew inside of me.

"That's fine, son. You are on your own. Go ahead and ruin your life. Just know that I have no intention of letting you ruin mine." He grabbed a jacket that I never realized he even took off and slid his arms into it as he walked toward the door grunting and groaning the entire way. "Odd though. Your young friend was very willing to never fuck you again," he said, stepping out onto the porch.

"Pardon me?"

He turned around, the porch light highlighting his furry eyebrows arched high on his forehead. "Lucy? That's her name, right? I paid her a visit earlier. Poor little thing was as nervous as whore in church. But, she's smarter than you. She will undoubtedly pay heed to my warning."

With zero hesitation, I lunged at my ruthless prick of a father, knocking him into the porch banister. "How dare you! Stay the fuck away from her," I gritted with his tie fisted in my hand. The urge to punch the smirk off his face almost won out.

His glare didn't bother me a bit. "Don't make me come up to New York again to deal with your shit." He jerked the front of his dress shirt, adjusting it back into place, then walked down the front steps.

After I slammed the front door behind me, I gave it a swift kick, trying to release a lifetime of frustration. I searched for my phone. I needed to call Lucy. When the doorbell rang again, I glanced around trying to figure out what my father had forgotten. My body still shook with rage, but I opened the door regardless.

Daryanne stood there in my old Princeton sweatshirt that I'd asked for twenty times, but I'd finally given up and let her keep.

"Seriously." As I tried to close the door, she stuck her arm in and shoved it open.

"I need to know one thing," she said. "Why her? Why not me?" Her whiney voice grated on my last nerve.

"Who told you where I lived?"

Her shoulder jetted up and down. She wasn't going to tell me. I was surprised she'd never knocked on my door before, honestly. There was no way my mood would tolerate an ounce of her shit.

"Daryanne. I'm not having the best of nights, could you please leave? I have some things I need to take care of."

"Jenner, please tell me. What is it that went so wrong?"

My entire body tensed when she grabbed the front of my sweatshirt like we were lovers. I grabbed her wrists, squeezing slightly and forcing her to let go, then I backed away from her. Her overwhelming perfume filled the distance between us.

"Nothing went wrong. We were just wrong. When you feel it, you feel it."

"And you feel it with her?"

"That's not what I'm saying. I'm saying I didn't feel it with you." My words were terse, but I didn't care.

My hand reached for the doorknob.

"Get out, Daryanne," I said as non-confrontational as possible and opened the door.

Lucy stood on my front step shivering. The tip of her nose was red, maybe from the cold, maybe from the tears. Her nose always reddened when she cried.

"Ms. Edwards." I hated the formality, but I was shocked.

A single rivulet of tears made its way from her eye down to her chin where it fell to her scarf. I wanted to hold her…to comfort her…and the only thing stopping me was Daryanne standing a mere ten feet away.

"Your father came to my apartment." She hiccupped a cry. "United States Supreme Court Justice Weber…he…"

I reached toward her, gripping her shoulders.

LUCY

My body hadn't stopped shaking from the moment Supreme Court Justice Weber walked out of my house. I hadn't shed a tear until Jenner opened the door. He had the right to know that his father had come by, the threats he'd made and my fear of never loving him again. We'd said the words, in my head I'd already said goodbye. Yet, as I stood before him, shivering from the cold, I wanted him to take me in his arms and tell me everything would be okay.

"Your father came to my apartment." I hiccupped a gasp. "United States Supreme Court Justice Weber…he came to my place." I shook my head, still in disbelief.

Jenner stood there. Frozen.

"Jenner," I whispered as a stream of tears strolled down one cheek.

Something was wrong. His vacant round eyes looked defeated. I wondered if the awful words I'd said to him to make him leave my apartment still resonated in his head. When he reached out, gripping my shoulders, my body stiffened.

"Lucy, listen to me. I need you to ignore what's going to happen in the next thirty seconds. I need you to know that I..."

Before he finished his sentence, Daryanne's blond curls came from the shadows. Inside. His. House. Daryanne.

I didn't know what Jenner was saying. Though I heard his words, no part of my mind could put them together. My life converted into a slow motion catastrophe playing out before my eyes. My eyes flickered to Jenner's as hard as I fought it. He shook his head as his mouth continued to move. All I could hear was blood swooshing in my ears as my heart crumpled.

She was there with him. At his house. They were together. I took two steps back, stumbling off the brick paved porch.

"Lucy. Lucy. Listen to me," Jenner raised his voice.

"It doesn't matter," I whispered. And it didn't. "It's ok."

Everything was stacked against us. We were wrong from the start. I had refused to believe it in the beginning. And I sure as hell didn't know what to believe at that point. The night had been an emotional rollercoaster, and I'd crashed. I needed to get away. My mind raced as my eyes moved back and forth between the two of them. I needed to compose myself. I needed to think. I needed out of there...so I left.

As I peeled my eyes open, I glanced at the window, looking for sunlight, hoping that the longest night in history was over. My nose was still stuffy from the night full of tears. And today was going to be no easier. It was funeral day. Paige Engle was being buried. She'd unfairly lost her battle with her mother's illness. Survivor's guilt hardened inside of me.

I slid my phone off the night table and unhooked the charger. Six missed calls. Three texts. All from Jenner.

Lucy, please call me.

I deserve the opportunity to explain

OK, it is your prerogative to disregard these texts but I'm asking you to please allow me to defend the circumstances. I understand your reaction.

The texts came in through the night, at different times. His night must have been as shitty as mine. Served him right. I wanted to respond but didn't know what to say. I decided to wait until after the emotional day played out. There was honestly no sense in carrying this on any longer.

There was no covering the red, rashly splotches on my face. Only time would help those disappear. And knowing more tears would be shed today, I applied very little eye-make up. Only some waterproof mascara…the rest of my face remained bare.

The funeral was small. A school bus sat out front of the funeral home; Paige's class must have come to say their goodbyes. Only a plant and a small arrangement of flowers sat on stands up by the…urn. She was cremated? I wondered about the autopsy Jenner mentioned. Immediately, anger raged inside my body. Cremation. How fucking ingenious. No investigation could be done after the fact. No evidence to charge her sick, bitch mother. As the thoughts registered through my brain, I spotted her. She wept—wails and literal howls of…grief. Or was it regret? Did she mean to kill her? I watched as people surrounded her. Consoled her. The kids from Paige's class simply stared at the spectacle.

The service was short; the urn was small, and the crowd was even smaller. My heart—already cracked and bleeding from the past few weeks—was simply crushed at the thought of what had happened to this poor girl. I wondered if she knew that her mother was hurting her or if she didn't understand the unjust hand she was dealt.

When I caught sight of the mother laughing in a corner, I couldn't think straight. The wrath I wished to unleash on this woman was justified but dangerous. At that moment I didn't care. Without thinking, I stood, and my feet started moving toward her. Suddenly, more than the rage,

I felt the magic floating through the air that I only sensed when Jenner was around. Two forces from extreme opposite ends of the emotional spectrum continued to propel me forward. A man, with his hand resting on Paige's mothers back, stared at me as I approached them. Unexpectedly, a hand intertwined with mine and led me in a different direction. The grip was strong, firm, unforgiving. But I knew his touch, and even though the hood covered his identity, I knew who he was.

As he casually led me away from my target, he remained silent. I knew his thoughts. I knew them before he even said them. He would reprimand me for attending the funeral. He would say that this shouldn't be personal. And, maybe it shouldn't be…but it was.

Once inside his car, we both sat staring out the windshield. The trees were almost completely stripped of their leaves. His hoodie still covered his head.

"Did the autopsy show anything?" I asked softly.

"I haven't heard anything, yet."

"But she was cremated. Isn't all evidence gone?" I shook my head, frustrated that we could have made a difference.

"Lucy, if it makes you feel better, feel free to blame me for this."

"Why didn't you trust me? Trust my instinct?"

A sarcastic huff of sardonic laughter scraped up his throat. "You really don't get it."

"No, Jenner. You don't get it!"

"I don't get it? Don't tell me I don't get it, Lucy." He yanked his hoodie off exposing his face. Obviously, he hadn't shaved in a while because the dark shadow of a beard covered his face. I hadn't noticed last night. "Have you ever looked into the eyes of a little Hispanic boy that had both palms burned on the kitchen stove because he stole his father's change jar to give to a kid at school so he wouldn't bully him anymore? I have! Have you ever looked into the eyes of a little girl who told the court she'd been hit with a horse whip but because DCF couldn't find one in the home, I had to put the little girl back into the home. The girl gets beat again and it isn't until she hides the horse whip in her backpack to show to her teacher that we realize she was saying a whore's whip. I've looked into her eyes too. Or there could be the seven-year-old boy whose father used a curling iron to penetrate him." I slammed my fist against the steering wheel. "You can't imagine the things I've seen in the short time I've done this job. Don't tell me I don't get it, Lucy. Don't fucking tell me that."

I knew my expression was all sorts of screwed up and my words fell silent.

"You shouldn't have come today, Lucy."

"It was the least I could do."

"You shouldn't have. It makes you look guilty." He shifted his car into drive.

"Guilty? I'm the one who was on her side."

"You still shouldn't have come."

"Are you talking about me coming to the funeral or to your house last night?"

His eyes closed as I watched his chest rise with an inhale. "That was unfortunate timing."

"Unfortunate timing? Is that what we're calling getting caught…says every guilty criminal."

"I'm not guilty, Lucy. My father paid me a visit. Then, she showed up. I thought he forgot something, and I opened the door. I never would have let her in."

Imitating his voice, I sarcastically repeated him, "she doesn't even know where I live. She's never been to my house. Take me to my car, please," I added in my own voice.

"Your car?"

"I drove Midge's car." I pointed at the black Honda Accord and gripped the door handle to get out as he parked next to it.

"I've clearly done a poor job showing you how I feel. I'm not sure you comprehend the gravity of…"

"Jenner," I interrupted. "Don't."

Jenner grabbed my hand. "Fine. OK. But, go home, Lucy. Please, if you've ever listened to me, don't go back in there. Just go home."

Once in the safety of my own car, I fell apart. My guts twisted into nauseous knots, and I had to take deep breaths just to keep from hurling. As stupid as it sounded, when Paige Engle was killed, a part of me died.

Losing Jenner was the initial blast, but her death was a reminder that I survived and what I was there to do. I still had so much to accomplish. The reality of doing it without him, though, seemed unimaginable. He'd become a part of my essence.

When I got back to my apartment, I dried my tears, changed my clothes and updated my resume with my short-term experience with the New York County District Attorney's office. To tell my future employer that I was wanting to move was going to be easier than telling them I got fired because I was sleeping with the judge. This job was so important to me that it was necessary that I pay heed to Jenner's father's warnings. If there was one person that would make sure that I never worked again, it would be him. Supreme Court Justice Weber made that perfectly clear. Leaving Jenner alone was going to be the hardest thing I'd ever done.

CHAPTER 19

SEQUESTERED

Jenner

For the next few weeks, I did everything in my power to give her the space she wanted. In court, I fought not to make eye contact, hoping she found comfort in the space. She didn't squabble when I ruled against the State. And, she hadn't been to my office even once. But I waited. Hoping.

That day, I woke to dry gin mouth. Trying to drown memories, I'd indulged in a few too many martinis last night. And now a severe ache seared through my head. Never had I utilized sick leave before, but I speculated today might be the day.

My phone rang as I sat at my desk contemplating my decision. At the same time I picked up the receiver, Larry walked into my office. I hadn't spoken to him since the night I left his house. He was undoubtedly the one who had informed my father about my questionable relationship. I understood. I wasn't mad at him. He was my chief judge and my father's friend.

"This is Judge Weber," I answered, holding up my index finger to Larry.

"Judge Weber? This is Wayne Collison from the Post."

I swallowed hard as my eyes darted up to Larry who literally plopped down in my office chair. "The Post?" he whispered.

I nodded.

"Sir, I was wondering if you'd like to comment on a piece we are running in tomorrow's paper."

"That depends on the nature of the piece," I answered. My eyes never left Larry's. His carried enough concern for the both of ours.

"Yes, sir. It's an article reporting that Your Honor participated in a love affair with a New York County assistant district attorney who served your division. Would you like to comment for the story, sir?"

"No. I have no comment. But I suggest you get yourself an attorney," I threatened.

"Judge Weber, we have a witness who is reporting such actions. Are you concerned that your cases shared with Ms. Edwards will be scrutinized by the appellate court?"

They knew it was Lucy… Fuck! A witness? Who the hell? Larry held up a piece of paper as he glanced down, pinching the bridge of his nose.

I read directly from it. "This story is a complete fabrication; therefore, I have no comment."

I disconnected the call, loosened my tie and regret soured my mouth instantly. This was a truth I wasn't going to get out of. I had no answers. None. This was not fabrication. The only thing I was sure of was Lucy.

Larry abruptly stood. "What the hell are we going to do?"

"How about you call 9-1-1."

Larry's jaw tightened ticking in and out as he ground his teeth. "God damn it, Jenner. This isn't just about you. This is also about your father. This is the integrity of this court system. This county."

"Has the Post contacted Lucy about this?"

Larry's eyes widened nearly bugging out of his head. "You're concerned about Lucy?"

"Yes, I am."

"If the news has wind of this story, she has probably already been fired."

"Shit!" I should have realized Daryanne wouldn't leave it alone.

"I'm going to call your father, Jenner. He needs to prepare and brace himself for this."

I stood, grabbing my cell phone from my jacket pocket. "You see Larry, you added in a fuck there that I didn't give."

My phone screen was blank. It had been blank for several weeks.

"I have to prepare a statement, Jenner. We have to stay ahead of this. Will you at least help me with that?"

"Stay ahead of it? I think we are a little too late on that. But, of course I will. My statement would begin with 'Daryanne Watkins should be fired. I'd had a relationship with Ms. Watkins prior to my judgeship. I ended things prior to beginning my judicial service. She reported this to the press as a jilted, rejected lover whose only motive was revenge. This had nothing to do with Lucy Edwards and she should be completely left out of the equation. Neither a case nor child was ever in jeopardy nor was any bias or favoritism shown. Lucy Edwards is a brilliant attorney who has the best interest of the child always at the foremost of her mind.'"

I smiled at Larry and the adversity in front of us. With caution, he reached over, touching my forearm.

"Jenner. You have the perfect little world. Please think about this before you blow it off."

I slid my arms into my suit coat. "The thing is Larry, this isn't really my world. It's the world that my father created for me."

There was no malice in my words to him. Unfortunately, Larry was having to deal with something that he shouldn't have to. And…that was my fault. Things were just becoming clearer every day to me.

As I left my office, my reputation, everything I'd thought was important to me was on the line. I knew that. But there was a bigger part of me that needed to make sure that Lucy was ok, and honestly, that trumped everything. Whether she wanted to see me or not, I was coming her way.

LUCY

The muscles in my arms burned as the boxes filled with the little bit of crap I'd accumulated in the five months I'd worked for the State. My eyes scanned the cars parked in the loading zone, but I didn't see Henley yet. I set the boxes down, giving my aching arms a break, glancing at my law books, the pictures in the frames and my law diploma…a short shelf life for all of them.

When the light rain began to fall, I simply closed my eyes. Things had only seemed to get worse for me as the weeks had drug on. People on the sidewalks began to scurry indoors, held newspapers over their heads and popped up umbrellas, though they didn't bode very well in the brutal, gale-force winds. Between the time Henley pulled up and parked and the time it took me to walk with boxes in tow to her car, I was soaked and frozen to the bone.

"Seriously?" she shouted, opening her trunk, then slamming it shut once I shoved the wet boxes inside. "She fucking fired you? What did he say? I thought you were going to quit."

I wasn't in the mood for the questions. Outside of feeling emotionally depressed, I was physically exhausted—to the point that all I wanted to do was crawl into bed. "I was going to quit. But I still don't have another job, and I was hoping to find one first. It's fine. My resume has been sent several places." I sighed, collapsing into her front seat.

"What a bitch. I can't believe she fired you. Though I would have fired you too."

"Thank you. Will you do me a favor?"

"Go beat her ass?"

I laughed, shaking my head. "Drive by the courthouse."

"Of course. Why?"

"Because it's perfect and symbolic of everything I just lost. When I walked up the steps of that courthouse the first time, something inside of me came alive."

"Yeah, so alive, you fucked the judge."

My hair was so wet that water streaked my face and dripped onto my clothes and off the tip of my nose. As we drove by the courthouse, I stared up at the ginormous pillars and steps leading up to them. "God, Henley. This all happened so fast. How did this happen?"

"I don't even have anything funny to say to that, Luce. This is crazy. This is like national news shit. Or at least Inside Edition or something. Scorned lover fires current lover of district court judge who happens to be the son of US supreme judge. Wicked news."

"Well, let's just thank God that it hasn't made the news. Better that the bitch fired me than telling the entire world."

Henley zigzagged through traffic as she drove me to my apartment. Once she parked out front, I sighed. "I'm going to the farm. Just for a bit."

"That's a long ways away."

"I know. I just really need to get my shit together. The farm is home. Honestly, I need to get away from him."

"Have you seen him?"

I shook my head; my heart racked with unbearable hurt. "No. Not since the funeral. I told him to stay away from me."

"That's good. He knows the two of you aren't right, too."

"What difference does it make now that I'm fired?"

Henley shrugged. "I guess none. But do you really believe that bitch just stopped by his house?"

I tilted my head to the side. "I don't know. I honestly don't know." I blew out a long breath. "I'll have my phone, but reception is a little spotty."

She nodded. "OK. I understand. Please keep me posted. OK?"

"I will."

"Promise?"

"I promise."

It didn't take me long to throw some clothes into a bag, gather a few personals, pack up my computer and shut things down in my apartment. I told Midge where I was going, and she agreed to take care of my mail plus keep an eye on the place. Being true to her character, she didn't ask anything, just embraced me with a tight, soothing hug. The smell of confections and joy clung to her.

I had to figure this thing called my life out. It was time.

Two days…that's how long it took for me to get settled and for the old farmhouse to feel like home. I spent the first day cleaning most everything, thinking about times spent with Pops. Thinking about our spring planting, summer crop, fall harvest and cold winters. A lifetime of memories spent with the best grandfather in the world. Sadly, only a shell of him existed now. I'd make a point to go into the city to see him tomorrow. The place Jenner had found for Pops was perfect. I never got to tell Jenner thank you. That sick feeling in my gut returned as thoughts of Jenner filled my head.

Still feeling exhausted and run-down, I'd not gotten out of my pajamas all day. I'd made a pot of chicken and noodles and mashed potatoes, and I ate until I was stuffed, sitting in front of the fire enjoying the smell of the burn and the sound of the crackling wood. When the doorbell rang, I shot upright. No one knew I was here. Except for Henley, and she would have called first.

I peeked out the side window, to see a man standing in the front porch light. His brows pulled together in confusion.

"Lucy?" he said, but I didn't really recognize him, I didn't think.

I opened the front door, knowing the screen door was locked. "Yes?"

"Damn girl. It's been a long time. It's me, Ethan. Hank's son."

Without reservation, I unlocked and opened the screen door. "Ethan! Oh my goodness." I threw my arms around his neck.

He'd gotten older, we all had, but he'd filled out and was a mini replica of Hank. Better looking even.

"Please come in."

He stepped into the house, his flannel shirt smelled like outdoors. His brown work boots were worn as were his faded jeans.

"What are you doing here?"

"Well, Dad's been staying with Cindy in town to stay as close to Pops as he can. So, I come here nightly to get the mail, check on the place and all. I was in the city last night and didn't make it by. What about you?"

I shrugged. "Life. Circumstance." I hid my pain with laughter.

"You always wanted to get to the city to be a hot shot attorney and now you're back here? I'm surprised. You look great by the way, Little Miss."

Ethan's crooked smile was the best welcome home present ever.

"Your eyes are sad," he said, walking past me to Pops' liquor cabinet. I watched as he spun the cap off the Jack. He poured two shots, then held one out to me.

After an exaggerated eye roll, I smiled and walked over and took it.

He held his glass, waiting to be clinked by mine. The whiskey burned all the way down till it collided with my stomach—and then came rushing right back up. I sprinted to the bathroom and barely made it to the toilet before hurling up the whiskey, and my dinner.

"You ok in there?" Ethan called from the living room.

"I'm fine," I called back, running water in my hands to rinse out my mouth. I caught a glimpse of my reflection in the mirror as I passed. Pale face. Dark circles under my eyes. God, I was a mess.

"Sorry about that. I guess I can't hold my liquor as well I thought."

Ethan just smirked and poured himself another shot. His eyebrows shot up in a question.

"Oh, no," I laughed. "I'm not about to put more of that whiskey in my stomach after that last shot." I sat down on the sofa and patted the seat next to me in silent request. Ethan obliged.

"You gonna tell me?" he asked, taking another drink.

"Not a lot to tell. I made a poor decision. Came out here to get lost for a bit."

"I doubt you made a poor decision, Little Miss. You overthought just about everything growing up. But I tell you what, if you want to get lost, this is the place to do it—as you ain't hidin'."

I bit down on the side of my cheek as I slid my feet beneath me on the sofa.

"What's his name?"

"Jenner."

"He hurt you?"

I had to think about that. "We hurt each other."

"You really want to talk about this?"

"No. Not particularly."

"Perfect. Me either," he laughed. "I'm the furthest thing from Dr. Phil. Claire and I can barely figure our own shit out." He laughed doing another shot.

"I'm sorry."

"I'm gonna head back anyway. How long you thinkin' 'bout stickin' around? Want me to come back tomorrow?"

He grabbed a throw off the chair and tossed it over me.

"I don't know how long I'll stay," I said, snuggling beneath it. "It feels really nice here right now. I could make dinner for us tomorrow night if you want to come back."

"Six?"

"Sure. Bring Claire?"

"Nah. I enjoy my own time here each evening." He winked.

"See you then."

He nodded as if he was tipping his hat in agreement. "I'll dead bolt the door. You stay put. Goodnight, miss," he whispered, leaning down and kissing the top of my head. I watched as he pulled the door closed and locked it.

"Goodnight," I said to the back of the door.

When I picked up my phone, I saw a voicemail from Jenner that had come in that morning. I didn't have a clue how I'd missed it but I wondered if reception kept it from coming in earlier.

Hi Lucy. I need you to call me. It's urgent.

First thing, I called to check on Pops. Hank said he was doing just fine. The only other thing it could be was that he'd heard about my termination. My guess was guilt was getting the best of him.

I pulled my knees up to my chest. Maybe my knees would help keep my heart from beating so forcefully. I hated that even the thought of Jenner seemed to cripple me. My exhaustion was starting to get the best of me, and though my old bed was calling me, I was pretty comfortable right where I was. Lying there, the only thing on my mind was Jenner. His touch. His smell. His taste. I missed him so much. I was an emotional wreck…tears invaded again.

The key turning in the lock brought me upright. Sunlight barreled in through every window. Ethan burst through the door along with a blast of frigid air. His angry eyes narrowed and his brows pulled together.

"What? Is it Pops?" I asked, panic shooting through me.

"No. This Jenner…he's a judge?"

I nodded, untangling myself from the throw and standing. How could one shot of whiskey make me feel like shit?

Ethan held out the newspaper. The Post. The headlines…oh God.

U.S. Supreme Court Justice Weber's Son's Judicial Indiscretions

My jaw fell slack as I literally collapsed on the sofa.

"The article names you, miss."

"Names me?" A sudden wave of nausea overwhelmed me. "How bad is it?"

Ethan strode over to me, yanking a chair out of the corner and sitting nearly knee to knee with me.

"It's bad, Lucy." He cleared his throat and read. "Blah blah blah… The Honorable Judge Jenner Weber carried on a romantic relationship with Ms. Lucy Edwards. Ms. Edwards, who is 9 years his junior, is fresh out of law school but not new to the judicial system. Ms. Edwards was the respondent in a child in need of care case out of Sullivan County. Ms. Edwards father is currently serving 13 years in the federal penitentiary for armed robbery. She has reportedly been terminated from the New York County District Attorney's office and was unable to be reached for comment."

Silent tears rolled down my cheeks as Ethan read my pathetic life in a nutshell of less than a paragraph.

"Did Jenner comment?"

The creases formed in Ethan's forehead could not be a good sign.

"His exact quote?" Ethan asked.

I nodded.

"This story is a complete fabrication," Ethan read verbatim, glancing up at me.

Those words completely stole the breath from my body. Everything inside of me deflated. He could have said no comment. He could have not said anything. But he said that we were a lie. A fabrication. He and I were an untruth as far as he was concerned.

"Lucy?"

At the sound of Ethan's voice, I remembered he was there. His eyes filled with pity. Ethan was as important to me as Hank. He'd been like

an older brother growing up. He was actually my first kiss—my only kiss—in the pumpkin patch out back. Only one time had he ever made fun of me—he'd made me cry when he said my mother was crazy. Hank would have none of that and took a belt to Ethan. Later that night, we both cried together after Hank made him apologize. He had held me then and now he took me in his arms once again. This time his arms were thicker, his chest broader, but his embrace was just as comforting.

I thought about Jenner's phone call yesterday and I couldn't help but believe that his message was to let me know what had happened. Maybe he was trying to give me the heads up. Maybe he was going to admit to being a gutless coward. As I cried with my cheek pressed against Ethan's chest, I wanted the inescapable hurt to roll away as freely as the tears. The pain seemed bound and determined to stick around, and I wasn't sure how much more I could take.

CHAPTER 20

ABSCONDER

Jenner

After ringing Lucy's bell with no answer, I resorted to knocking and then obnoxiously pounding. I didn't care if I upset her. We needed to talk.

"Lucy! Come on. Open up. I know you're in there."

I rested my head against the wood door. Waiting. Hoping. Praying.

"She's not in there."

I spun around. Lucy's neighbor, the baker, stood across the hall with the door open.

"Where is she?"

The lady glared at me with that damn rolling pin in her hand as she waved it in what I could assume was an unfulfilled threat. What was it with this rolling pin?

"Please," I added desperately. "You have to tell me."

"The newspaper said nothing ever happened between you two, so I'll pretend this didn't happen as well," she said, slamming the door in my face.

Touché…That old bird was tough. I might normally admire her spunk, but right now I was pissed that she gave me nothing. She knew exactly where Lucy was. I inhaled deeply trying to gather my muddled thoughts. When I stepped out of the brownstone apartment building, two men with cameras started snapping pictures of me, taking the stairs two at a time.

"Judge Weber! What did Ms. Edwards say about the allegations?"

I stepped past them, unlocking my car.

"Judge. Does your father have a comment regarding the most recent allegations?"

When I shut the door, their voices muted. Thank God. My father would be so pleased that there was now evidence of me going to see her. I turned on the radio, drowning out their voices and my thoughts. Next stop Henley Callaway. She'd already let me have it at Tony's Tavern telling me to stay away from Lucy. My guess—she would be unwilling to give me any information either. But, I had to try.

The girl lived in a nicer neighborhood than Lucy. The lights were on in her apartment as dusk settled, and once I'd parked, I didn't hesitate to sprint up to the porch. Moments later, when she opened the door to my knock, her face hardened instantly.

"Wow."

"You're her best friend. I need to find her."

With pursed lips, Henley propped her hand on her hip. I seriously didn't have time for this.

"Please," I added.

"She wants to be left alone."

I nodded. "I understand. But, I need to talk to her."

"Why? According to your story, nothing was going on. Why would you need to talk to her?"

I blew out a long, slow breath. This was not going to get me anywhere. "Look, Henley. I fucked up. Please, if you speak with her, tell her I'd like to talk to her."

I didn't wait for her response.

Back in my car, I decided I'd do the one thing I didn't want to do. I texted her.

I'd like to speak with you.

I sent the text while stopped at a stoplight and by the time I'd gotten home, I'd still heard nothing. Using any professional contacts to find out what I needed was out of the question given what was happening in the news. But I needed help to find her. After four long minutes passed, I sent another text.

Please.

It's not that texting wasn't a valuable means of communicating, it was. But I'd seen so many cases where texting records and actual texts had led to a conviction. As I sprawled out on the sofa, my body ached. Maybe I was coming down with something. I closed my eyes thinking back about the night I'd met her. That night at the club. Rarely did we even go there, but Jeff wanted to hit the club. Looking back, I should have known she was a virgin. She had virgin written all over her. The comments Henley made that grabbed my attention to begin with. The blood that invaded Lucy's innocent cheeks. *Tell me what to do*, Lucy said. How easy it was to make her come. How tight she felt. I didn't pay a lick of attention to the condom when I pulled it off or the sheets beneath us. God, how I wanted a do-over. The one thing I did know... where Pops was staying. She'd come there to see him soon enough.

CHAPTER 21

ADMONISHMENT

Lucy

The entire trip into the city, Ethan and I talked about Claire and Jenner. He and Claire had so much more history than Jenner and I. He and Claire had been together for as long as I could remember. High school sweethearts. Jenner and I—we were electric from the start. Mimi always said love was the closest thing to magic, and after I met Jenner, I believed that. There was definitely magic in the way he touched me without using his hands. His words. His eyes. His honesty. His stupid wealth words. I smiled as I sat shotgun in Ethan's truck. I missed Jenner's big words.

"Why not text him back? The reason you were staying apart is gone now." Ethan asked.

"Ethan. I have no idea if he is in trouble. If he will be going before an ethics committee. I had a United States Supreme Court Justice in my living room. Complete asshole, by the way. This whole thing blew up in our face—just exactly like we feared."

"Do you love him?"

"Yes, but it is more complicated… Pull over, now!" I shouted, unlocking and opening my door before Ethan came to a complete stop. I vomited my breakfast all over the shoulder of the road.

Ethan grabbed a napkin from his console and handed it to me.

"Lucy, are you ok?"

I nodded silently. Damn I was tired of this bullshit.

"Probably just all the nerves right now." I wiped my lips and took a deep breath of air, trying to settle my still roiling stomach.

Ethan just stared at me. Assessing me like the crops we took to market.

"What?" I asked, a little put off by his serious expression.

"Don't take this the wrong way, Little Miss," Ethan said evenly, forcing me to hold his gaze. "But is there any chance you might be pregnant?"

The shock of his question stole the answer that came immediately to my head. I wiped my bottom lip again as his question ricocheted around in my head.

No. Not possible. But…I had been exhausted lately. And nauseous all the time. Shaking my head in denial, I grabbed my phone and scrolled through my calendar to when I marked my last period. Mid September. My eyes glanced at the date at the top of my phone. November 18. Crap!

I started scrolling again, this time looking at the dates Jenner and I had been together at the conference.

Stomach acid scorched the back of my throat as I searched frantically for the dates. October 5. Holy fuck me.

"Ethan…" I whispered.

He grabbed my hand and gave it a squeeze. "It's ok. Nothing is certain. Let's get a test and then you'll know."

"I can't. Ethan. I can't."

Henley's comment about me being pregnant with the judicial spawn rang through my ears. Was that even a possibility?

I relived that night over in my head as I sat there in shock. I vividly recalled watching Jenner first undress me, then undress himself. After he went down on me, I remembered him crawling on top of me almost immediately, then slowly burrowing himself inside of me. My entire body quaked as I thought about that moment…that night. In my subconscious, I knew he hadn't put on a condom. And in the heat of the moment, I wasn't about to ask him to stop. Even laying there after he'd finished, I felt the wetness…our wetness… between my legs, and I hadn't given it a second thought. I wasn't mad at him for not having protection. I was more irritated with myself for not thinking this could even be a possibility.

I'd never been on the pill. I'd never needed it. Now it was too late to take the morning after—hell, I needed the month after pill.

Ethan had started driving again.

"I never wanted kids," I whispered.

He glanced over at me then back to the road. "Why?"

"Because of my mother. Well, and my father too, I guess. I have the world's worst genes. Severe mental illness. Criminality."

"Lucy. We aren't our parents."

"How do you know? My mother seemed to have a fairly normal life until she had me. What if something clicks inside of you one day and you just start hurting your child or those around you?" My voice cracked.

"You're being silly, Miss. You'd never hurt a fly."

Looking for relief, I turned the temperature knob down for some cooler air.

Twenty more minutes of running what-if scenarios through my head convinced me that I was indeed pregnant. Somehow, I just knew. And the rest of the trip, I sat quietly thinking about my options. No matter how many options were out there...I knew there was only one for me.

I cried on the way to Pops and I cried in the truck on the way home. The visit didn't go anything like I'd hoped. Nothing in my life at this point has gone like I'd hoped. Jenner was the best thing that had happened and that had only lasted about a week before I realized who he was and what that meant for us.

As Ethan and I road in silence, I thought about the things Jenner had said. He was so very right—I never would have gone into those Judge's chambers on either occasion had I not slept with him. I wouldn't have challenged him on any level.

Being a child in need of care prosecutor was everything I'd ever wanted, and I would never have jeopardized my career...until I met Jenner.

When Ethan shifted the truck into park, I glanced out the windshield. He'd parked in front of a drug store.

"Want me to go in and buy it or do you want to?"

"I can go."

"Why don't we both go?"

I smiled at him. "Deal."

As we walked through the aisles, Ethan stayed close.

"I know it isn't any of my business and I may sound older brotherish, but you should've used protection, Miss."

The irony of that statement was not lost on me.

"Yep, just my luck. Jenner and I only had sex twice, once without protection, and here I am. Stupid, I know."

"You two only had sex twice?"

I nodded as my eyes scanned the variety of pregnancy tests. Wow, there were a lot. Didn't know if I wanted a plus sign, or 2 lines, but I went with the one that flat out spelled pregnant. Nothing lost in translation there.

I shrugged, a little embarrassed about where this conversation was headed. "My only two times ever actually. What are the odds of getting pregnant your second time out of the shoot?" I grabbed one of the boxes.

"Wait. You and he had sex twice or you've only ever had sex twice?"

"Yes." I shook the box of the one I chose.

"You were a virgin until you slept with this guy?"

I nodded. "Just my luck."

"Do you even like this guy?"

"First time around, I barely knew him. It was just about the sex. No judging! I was done being the only virgin left in the world. Second time around, I was falling pretty hard for him. See if this helps with your understanding. He is the nicest, funniest, wittiest, handsomest, prick judge I've ever met."

Ethan chuckled a deep belly laugh. "Sounds like true love."

After we'd paid and gotten back on the road, the reality hit me. Tonight, or tomorrow morning, I'd know if my entire life was changing. If the one thing I never wanted to be—was going to be.

JENNER

Pops' appearance was worse than the night I'd seen him in the emergency room. He sat staring vacantly out the window at the birds flying around the birdfeeders.

I cleared my throat to draw his attention, wondering if he was lucid today.

"Hi, Pops."

"Hello."

I stepped into the room.

"Forgive me, I sometimes don't remember people the way I should."

I extended my hand, moving toward his wheel chair.

"We've not met, sir. Not officially anyway. I'm Jenner. I'm a friend of Lucy's."

His eyes narrowed just a bit. If someone hadn't been looking for it, they may not have noticed.

"Nice to meet you. How do you know my granddaughter?"

The continual thud of my heartbeat was resounding in my throat. "I'm in love with her, sir. I've spent the last five months getting to know her. I just wanted you to know that I'm going to take care of her."

"Why hasn't Lucy told me about you?"

"I don't think she knows how much she loves me yet. Our relationship has been a little complicated, and I've made a few mistakes along the way." God that was an understatement. "It won't be today, and probably not tomorrow or maybe not even this year, but I plan to ask her to marry me. It would be my hope that when that time comes, I could have your blessing."

"I'm confused. Why didn't she come with you?"

I sat next to him. I didn't want to lie to him. I didn't know what he might possibly remember. "I am a judge and Lucy worked for me. We found each other before either of us knew that. Things have kind of gone haywire, and I've lost her for a bit. But, I love her, Mr. Walker. I love her."

The elderly man's face crumbled as his frail hand reached out for mine.

"Ethan. Find Ethan. He will help. He loves her too. She's so darn stubborn."

Ethan? A single tear found its way down the maze of wrinkles on his face.

"Who is Ethan," I asked jealousy coursing through every vein, artery, and cell in my body.

Pops stared out the window again.

"Mr. Walker. Who is Ethan?"

"My dad died."

My eyes closed. I couldn't lose him. Not now. Not when I was so close to finding her.

"I love her," I repeated.

His vacant eyes shot up toward my face. Shit. I'd lost him.

"I'm sorry. Do I know you?"

I shook my head, frustrated and sad. "No, sir. Just checking on you. You need anything?"

"My granddaughter is coming today."

I gave him a comforting smile. His love for Lucy held no bounds. I wouldn't let him down. Ever.

After a four-hour stakeout in my car waiting for Lucy to possibly show, I left the facility and drove to her apartment—where once again, I knocked repeatedly. The older lady across the hall must not have been home. No rolling pin. No smart-ass remarks. Desperate, I placed my ear on the door but heard nothing. Henley. I wondered if she was staying there. Hiding out.

Staring out the window of the train, I gazed past the snow-dusted trees, completely lost in thought. I barely even noticed the sparkling light dancing off of the branches or the winter birds fluttering about searching for seeds. There was very little that excited me these days. Five weeks had passed since I'd gone to see Pops. The five longest weeks of my life. After following every lead I could think of, I still had no idea who this Ethan was, but I hoped he wasn't spending his nights with her. Just thinking about that possibility made me see red. Christmas was three days away. I'd fought to stay in my routine. Otherwise I would go crazy. Thankfully, the judge sex scandal was old news, at least in the media. Probably because Lucy was completely missing in action, making it lose its juicy news value. All of my transcripts and recordings from the past few months were under review. Honestly, I didn't care, but my father cared enough for both of us. I thought it would grow easier not seeing her, not hearing from her, but the crack in my heart became a canyon.

The two-hour trip on the train to DC wasn't how I'd planned to spend my day, but I was done playing games. I was done with everything it seemed except her. It's amazing how losing something precious to you can put your life into perspective. My father had no problem showing up at my door on a whim. This time, I was going to his.

Grace had been his assistant for as long as I could remember. When she saw me duck through the door, her eyes smiled before her mouth.

"Jenner!" she whispered with a shushed enthusiasm. "My, oh my. Look at you, handsome boy. Does he know you're coming?" she asked as she hugged me—all enthusiasm gone from her tone.

"Hi, Grace." I hugged her back, ashamed for not at the very least giving her a heads up. "No. He is not expecting me."

She tsked as she glanced at his schedule. "Jenner. You know that he doesn't like…"

"Me? Yes, I know."

"That's not what I was going to say. Interruptions. He doesn't like interruptions."

As I walked toward his door, I faked a grin. "I think he dislikes me more than interruptions." I winked, hoping to alleviate some anxiety.

"He loves you. He just isn't good at showing it, and this stuff in the news, you have to understand…"

"I do," I interjected and opened his door.

He looked up from whatever he was reading, peering over his thick reading glasses. Immediately, he sat back in his massive chair and tilted his head to the side, staring at me in that intense way that always set me on edge. Always the judge.

"Well. Well. Well. As I live and breathe, my son steps into the halls of justice." He tossed his glasses onto the desk. He was one damn smug son of a bitch. "Let me guess. You're done with the girl, don't want to be appealed, and you are looking for guidance."

"From you? Not a chance in hell. But I do expect help."

"With regards to?"

"Lucy." I waited for his lame reaction.

Only a deep breath. "What do you want, Jenner?"

"You'll need a piece of paper to write this down."

He didn't move.

"You will help develop and implement a private foundation for abused children."

"Why would I do that?"

"She lost her job. Her life. Because of me. And *we* are going to extend her an opportunity."

His hands ran the length of his face.

I continued, "Don't act all put out by this. Someone will reach out to her by cell phone to request she apply for the director and legal advisor of the foundation. You will put together a small board to oversee it."

"Why would I do this?"

"Because I asked you to. Because you had no right to pay her a visit. Because I love her."

"Then you do it."

"No...I can't have any ties to it."

Confusion colored his face. "There will be a tie. I'm your father."

Holding up a finger, I said, "Albeit a terrible one. This is your chance for redemption. You have connections. You know people who can pull this off and who can fund it. You have people eating out of your damn ass. Make. It. Happen."

For the first time in a long time, I could see him mulling over my words as he leaned back in his massive chair.

"Fine. Let me see what I can do."

"She was making about $65k with the county. I'd love to see that doubled."

"Glad you aren't asking for much," he said with sarcasm, shaking his head.

"I gotta go," I added as I turned back to the door. "It was good to see you...Dad."

I could feel his eyes burning a hole through my back. The name Dad hadn't come out of my mouth in many years. Like, maybe since the Da-

da stage. The jab left me feeling victorious. As I walked out, my smile for Grace was much more genuine. She blew me a kiss, and I caught it.

CHAPTER 22

REBUTTAL EVIDENCE

Lucy

"Oh, Lucy. I'm so sorry." Claire held my hair as I hurled into the toilet again.

Ethan and his wife had been a godsend. Pregnancy didn't agree with any part of my mind or body. Claire came over to help me when my days were bad. It was another bad day. I'd wept enough tears over the past few weeks to fill the Hudson. My abs screamed from the tightening that came along with the daily retching.

I sat upright. "Claire, you don't have to stay. I'll be fine."

"You are so weak, girlie. I'm worried about you."

Finding my balance, I staggered to the sink to wash my mouth out. "Seriously, you can go. You have your own things you need to take care of. I'll be fine. This stupid morning sickness shouldn't be as bad the rest of the day."

I grabbed my Ensure shake from the fridge and collapsed on my makeshift bed on the sofa.

"Lucy," Claire whispered as she picked up my feet, so she could sit beside me. Even though the foot rub felt good, I cringed because I knew what was coming. "Jenner deserves to know you are pregnant."

I closed my eyes, hoping to hide my reaction to hearing his name. After all these months, my chest still felt as if it was caving inward making it impossible to breathe. Right after I'd left, Jenner had reached out several times…but still angry and frustrated, I'd blown him off. Never returned a call, or his texts. I didn't know what to even say to him at the time. And now… fear of his rejection consumed me. I wasn't a solo act anymore. Every decision I made from here forward affected this tiny creature in my womb.

Henley texted me regularly. For almost a month straight it seems, Jenner had showed up at her place looking for me. The last text I'd gotten from him was a *Merry Christmas* message…that was a month ago.

"Claire. I know he deserves to know. I get it. But Henley says our cases are almost done being reviewed. I don't want to mess that up. Plus, I'm sure he just wants this to be over. And the last thing he needs is a baby thrown into the mix." I recollected our conversation about not wanting children. A surge of nausea overwhelmed me again and I ran to the bathroom dry heaving into the toilet.

Claire rounded the corner. "I'm sorry. I shouldn't have brought it up. Don't tell Ethan I said anything."

"Why? Ethan agrees with you."

"Yes, but he worries about you being upset. You're his first love, you know. He will always like you better."

I laughed, wiping the spit dangling from my lower lip.

"He likes me because I'm not his wife. He likes me because I don't control his penis."

Claire laughed out loud. "True. But, he has always adored you."

Her words filled my heart. I thought back about those hateful words uttered by Papa Supreme that night at my apartment telling me I wasn't good enough for his son. Those words continued to haunt me. I was more than good enough. It was my family baggage that was the deal breaker.

"Want me to call the gal and postpone your interview for the foundation?"

I shook my head, then clipped up my hair. "No. I'm going to go. The trip into the city isn't a problem. I'm just nervous about possibly running into him."

"That isn't likely, Miss."

I huffed a laugh. "Let me tell you what's not likely, Claire. It's not likely to find a guy in a club, take him home, have him strip you of your virginity, then walk into the courtroom where you are just starting a new job and BAM!" I shouted. "You realize you slept with the judge. BUT! It happened. Regardless of how unlikely it might be."

Claire giggled, sliding her arms into her jacket sleeves. "Sounds like fate to me. I mean, come on, Miss. This has Hallmark movie ending written all over it."

I scrunched my nose at her. "My life is more like One Flew over the Cuckoo's Nest meets Law and Order."

"You deserve happiness, Lucy. You deserve him. I wish you'd realize that," Claire added, changing the tone of the conversation.

At that moment, the slightest movement fluttered down low in my belly —so soft and mild that I questioned if I'd really felt it.

JENNER

I couldn't remember a time in my life where I'd been more confused. Every single case Lucy and I shared had been reviewed and none of them had been appealed or overturned. My credibility had been questioned, and I'd come out on top. Yet confusion and unhappiness joined forces at my door. Maybe it was because my life had basically stayed the same and hers was turned completely upside down.

A month and a half had passed since my father told me he'd set up the foundation. It seemed like it was going to happen. One of the donors had contacted Lucy trying to arrange an interview. Apparently, she was interested in the position.

On Valentine's Day—a highly overrated Hallmark holiday— I don't know what drove me to go by Lucy's apartment again, but something told me she was there. I knocked softly, not wanting to bring out any rolling-pin brandishing neighbors. When I heard movement inside the apartment, it was as if a balloon that had filled my chest for the past four months popped, allowing me to finally breathe.

When the door opened, my heart dropped. It wasn't Lucy. The short, blonde standing in the doorway raised her brows. "Yes?"

"May I speak to Lucy?" My eyes searched the opening behind her.

"She's not here."

I pushed right past the girl. "Lucy!"

"Oh my God. Who are you? Lucy isn't here."

The girl ran past me and grabbed her cell phone.

"Lucy!" I shouted again as I darted from room to room.

"Get out!" she shouted. "I am subletting this place from her. She's not here!"

Subletting? "Where is she?"

"I don't know!"

"Can you come with me?" The voice drew both of our attentions.

Rolling pin lady stood in the doorway. Shit!

"You. Come." She pointed at me with that damn rolling pin, then walked through the doorway across the hall. I followed. The smell of sugar and kindness met me at the door.

"Sit down."

I did.

"Listen to me, young man. You can't do that. You can't just bust through someone's door. She's not here, and she's not coming back for a while."

I swallowed hard, the balloon in my chest filled to capacity again. "Where is she?"

"I can't tell you that."

"Can't or won't?"

"That's semantics."

She picked up a sifter and sprinkled powder sugar over a plate of some type of dessert bars.

"Would you get her a message for me?"

"No need to. She's getting yours just fine."

I watched as she pulled out some sort of saran wrap, tore it off, then placed it over what she'd just made.

"Who is Ethan?"

As she guided a few stray hairs off her forehead with the back of her hand, she shrugged and carried the plate toward me.

"Lucy told me a few months ago that you loved key lime. I made

163

these for someone else, but you take them. Happy Valentines." She winked.

"Where is she? Is she ok?"

She sat across from me, wiping her hands on her apron.

"Young man. Let me tell you something. That beautiful girl never felt wanted by her psycho of a mother. Even less by a father who cared more about money than family. Honestly, I think she sometimes felt like even her grandfather took her in because he had to. But he loved her more than anyone ever could. When she went off to college and then law school, she pretty much cut herself off from the real world. Threw everything into her studies. She had a dream, you see. And then, the moment she was willing to let down her guard a little and open herself up, you were there. I'm pretty sure you'd be the first to admit that your relationship with Lucy wasn't exactly fairytale material. I think your actions, reactions, once again left her feeling unwanted. From what I have read in the papers, and in Lucy's texts, I understand why you probably did what you did. But, shame on you. She deserved so much more."

I lowered my head ashamed. I didn't need her making me feel bad, I felt that way all on my own.

"I'll make this right. It's killing me every day how I handled that whole mess."

At the door, with my key lime bars in hand, I offered her a sturdy nod. "Thank you. Thank you for having her back."

Knowing Lucy had told Midge about my messages, I knew I had nothing to lose. That night at home, sitting in front of a fire that I wished I was sharing with her, I texted.

Lucy-I'm sorry.

My eyelids grew heavy as I kept my phone in my hand, willing it to vibrate. The flames from the fireplace splayed out shadows across the room in a hypnotic pattern, lulling me to sleep. I hadn't really slept well for months, but something about Midge's kindness gave me hope.

I shot upright off the sofa to the ring of my phone. I didn't recognize the number, but there wasn't a chance in hell I was going to miss Lucy if it was her.

"Hello?"

"Jenner?"

"Yes."

"Good morning. This is Janelle Iliff."

"Good morning, Janelle. How are you?" I wanted to shout 'have you talked to Lucy' but I didn't.

"I'm fine. Thank you. I know it's Saturday, but I was wondering if you could meet for coffee. I spoke with the young lady we interviewed."

"Is she taking the position?"

"I think so. At least she is considering. However, there are some concerns."

"What concerns?" I bee-lined it for the bedroom, undressing as I walked.

"That's what I wanted to speak with you about."

"Ok, that's fine. Thirty minutes? Tell me where." I turned the shower on.

"How about the sidewalk café over in the village? I need an hour."

Thirty minutes longer than I wanted, but that would have to do.

"I'll see you there. Thank you."

I jumped in the shower, ecstatic that in sixty minutes I might know how to find Lucy. Things were looking up. I inhaled the deepest of breaths. Everyone deserved a second chance but never for the same mistake. Once I had her back, I would never hurt her again. Ever.

The café was busier than I'd expected, and I waited impatiently for Janelle to arrive. I stood as she approached.

"Nice to officially meet you, Jenner," she said as she extended her hand.

We shook hands, and then sat at a little table in the corner of the room.

"To you, as well. What's going on?"

"OK. So, we met with Ms. Edwards, and she is considering the offer to head up the foundation. Some members of the board questioned her qualifications, but we deflected them or answered them discreetly. Your father asked that the interview process be completely confidential with regards to your name or his being associated with it," she said with raised brows.

"That's correct."

"Your father said you wanted a copy of all the paperwork. This is the generic interview form we used to gather her information."

Without thinking, I spun the paper around, getting high at simply seeing that familiar handwriting. My eyes found the address line as I committed it to memory.

"...that's going to be costly, I'm sure. So, though we offered her the position, that was one of the main concerns I had."

I glanced up at her. "I'm sorry. I didn't hear that first part. What is the concern?"

"Health care. She's going to need it."

"No problem. She's single. It won't be that costly." That was the last of my worries.

"With all due respect, Jenner, prenatal care is expensive."

Blood drained from my head, causing my thoughts to swim. I shook my head, trying to force the tunnel vision away.

"Pardon me?"

"Ms. Edwards is pregnant. I believe she said four or five months along. I can get clarification. Even though we have offered her the position, we can certainly express that we've reconsidered and retract the offer."

Janelle's mouth continued to move. The only thing running through my mind at the moment was that night in the hotel room when I didn't have a condom. Our skin was already magnetic when it touched, but that night as I slid inside of Lucy, it was magical. And being able to come inside of her was not just a first for me but for her as well. Jesus.

I'd planted a seed that night.

"Jenner?"

I swallowed, unable to find words as a mixture of emotions swelled inside of me. I vacillated between jumping up and running or finishing the conversation. Is that why she'd stayed away? My mind fought with thoughts of what was going through her head as well. Was she never going to tell me?

"Jenner, what do you want me to do?"

I cleared my throat. "Nothing. Nothing yet. I need to check on a couple of things." I stood, knowing full well how rude I was being. "I'll call you." And...I left.

Chapter 23

Deliberation

Jenner

Two hours, that's how long it took me to navigate my way to the address. How it never occurred to me that she would return to the home she shared with Pops surprised me. Honestly, I didn't even know if this was the house she was raised in, but seeing the cropland next to the beautiful, old farmhouse, I suspected it was. After abruptly bailing on Janelle, I had only shot home long enough to change clothes, figure out where I was going and hit the road. Now, here I was. Still not sure what I would say when I saw her.

When I turned down the drive, I drove slowly, watching for shadows in the house. Lights were on and two big trucks sat in the gravel circle in front of the house. Dusk had settled, and as I got out of the truck, I grabbed the flowers sitting shotgun. After a long, slow, deep breath, I scaled the porch steps. A porch swing swayed in the winter breeze, and I pictured Lucy and me on it.

My hand shook as I reached for the doorbell finally ringing it. The nerves had nothing to do with my being here—they were completely dependent on her reaction.

When the door opened, it wasn't Lucy's eyes I stared into, but rather the steely glare of a tall, somewhat handsome man. No greeting just that glare. He examined me from head to toe.

"May I speak with Lucy, please?"

He glanced over his shoulder, licked his lips, then stepped aside allowing me entry. She was here. I was going to see her. Finally.

"Ethan? Who is it?" her voice chimed from somewhere in the house.

So, this was Ethan. I wasn't sure if I wanted to beat his ass or not. That verdict would be held in abeyance. But I sure as hell sized him up as I stood next to him. He closed the front door with an eerie softness, perhaps controlling his own emotion.

"I'm Jenner. I'm a friend of Lucy's." I extended my hand.

Ethan puffed a sarcastic huff, shaking his head, and with tight lips he shook my hand with a forceful grasp. My upper lip pulled up just a bit.

A pretty blonde rounded the corner with a small child in her arms.

"Oh, God!" She froze, staring at me, then wedged herself between us facing Ethan. "We have to go. Now. Ellie is so fussy," she lied, bouncing the smiling girl on her hip.

Ethan walked past me, and I followed him. I wasn't sure if he was leading me to Lucy or not, but I sure the fuck wasn't going to back down from this man.

"Ethan," the lady behind me said with a warning in her tone.

"Hey E. Who was at the door?"

I rounded the corner as Lucy asked the question, and her eyes fell over me. Shock plagued her expression. Judging by the smells wafting from the delicious-looking country spread, it was dinnertime. The table where she sat hid her body from view.

I offered her a tight-lipped smile. Imagine a treasure hunter trying to hid his joy at finding a treasure. That was me as I stood there masking all emotion.

"Jenner." My name brushed over her lips; disbelief colored her tone.

Ironic. I controlled the fate of others in my courtroom, and yet I had absolutely no control over my own future. It all rested with her. She was the judge and jury that would seal my fate. I had to let her know that I wanted a life sentence.

"Hello, Lucy."

"We were just leaving, Lucy," The blond woman said. "You two enjoy dinner. Ellie is super fussy, and we just need to get home."

The child giggled, bringing a lopsided grin to my own face. Lucy stayed seated, but her stare slid over to Ethan, who rested his clinched fists on the table.

"Ethan," the woman with the child gritted her teeth.

Ethan simply stared at Lucy until she nodded. I wasn't sure what the connection was, but it certainly was there. As hard as it was to drag my eyes away from Lucy, I met Ethan's hostile gaze. He didn't say anything. Just sized me up. Obviously fighting some internal struggle. Finally, heaving a resigned sigh, he swaggered past me. If things went the way I hoped, maybe someday Ethan and I would eventually be on the same team.

My eyes slid back to Lucy.

"Hi," I greeted again.

"Hello."

Once the front door closed, I held up the flowers. "Vase?"

"Under the sink," she said, not budging.

I slid the flowers into the glass and set them on one end of the table.

"Thank you. What are you doing here?"

"Well, you sort of just disappeared."

"Gosh. That seems so long ago."

"Not that long ago."

"How'd you find me?" she said quietly.

I shrugged. "I finally put two and two together, but it took me a while."

"Was it Midge? I heard you got some key-lime bars." A hint of a smile touched her lips.

I stayed standing. I was going to force her to stand. To let me see her belly. "No. Midge kept your secret. She's very loyal to you. I heard you were getting my messages."

"Jenner, don't. Please."

I rested my head back against the wall. "You have goose bumps on your arms. It's cold in here, Lucy. Why are you wearing a tank?"

"I was cooking, and I got warm. My shirt is right there."

The plaid shirt was less than three feet from her, but she would have to stand up to reach it, and I knew damn good and well she wasn't going to stand.

"Will you hand it to me, please."

"No."

Her jaw tensed. The tight tank top showed off her breasts nicely.

"Your nipples wouldn't be as easy to see if I get you that shirt."

Blood crept into her cheeks as her lips parted. Her gaze fell down to the empty plate in front of her. I grinned. I had hoped and prayed on the drive up here that seeing me and hearing my words might provoke a positive response versus a text. I couldn't wait to make her mine again.

"Jenner." My name flew past her lips so beautifully.

"Are you staying here alone?"

Two of her fingers rested on her lips. "Yes."

I glanced down the hallway at the framed pictures of her on the wall. Her red mane seemed more wild back then.

"Who is Ethan?"

"Hank's son."

Of course. "And that was his wife?"

"Yes."

"He seemed quite protective of you. He knows who I am?"

She nodded. "Yes."

Our eyes connected again and held onto each other.

"How did you find me?"

"I already told you, Lucy. Can't you at least stand up and give me a hug?" I asked, fighting a smile.

God, she was honestly the most beautiful thing I'd ever seen. Her red hair fell perfectly around her shoulders. When her chin quivered, and she buried her face into her palms—as cute as it was—my heart wreaked havoc in my chest.

I took my time getting around the table, not wanting to startle her. Her face was still hidden in her hands, and I took hold of her wrists.

"Jenner," she whispered, resisting me.

"Let me hold you, please." I needed to hold her as much as I needed to breathe.

Finally, she conceded. Her body immediately melted into mine and she wept. Her body shook, and for a short second mine did too as my own eyes flooded. I'd found her…

LUCY

My entire body quaked, but Jenner's strong arms supported me. I still couldn't wrap my mind around the fact that he was standing in my kitchen. My tears drenched his shirt. And, I had no idea how long he'd stay. He held me like his life depended on it, and that thrilled me to the bone. But, it was only a matter of time before he saw the bump.

He brushed a kiss over the top of my head, then gripped my shoulders, pushing me back. I got lost in the wetness of his lashes, forgetting for just a second about the baby. But then his eyes widened in disbelief, his hands moving to brush the bare skin where my tank had ridden up. I so wanted him to choose me…us. I was an us now.

"Jesus," he whispered, falling to his knees. He laid his check on the roundness of my belly as a single tear streaked his cheek. "I knew, Lucy. I could feel it when you left. You, literally, took a part of me with you. And not just this baby, but my heart too."

I clawed at his hair, desperate for his approval and love. After all this time. After fighting to forget. After talking myself out of telling him. I fell right back into his arms.

His hands gripped my hipbones possessively. He was the only man I'd ever been intimate with and just that smallest of gestures aroused me. My nipples protruded even more now than when he had made his earlier comment.

"Lucy. My beautiful Lucy. How far along are you?" He spoke directly to my belly.

"It was the night in the hotel, Jenner. Five months. I didn't know before I left, and I didn't know how to tell you after things got so bad. But, Jenner, you can't talk me out of keeping this baby."

Several different expressions crossed his face before he settled on confusion.

"Why would I talk you out of keeping it? Don't be ridiculous."

"You don't want kids. You told me that. You made that very clear."

He nodded. "Yes. I told you that. But, that was before."

"Before what?"

"Before I knew what I was missing. Before I found you. Before I fell in love with you. Before I lost you."

His words gutted me—left me unable to breathe. I pushed away from him.

"What, Lucy? What?"

"You can't say stuff like that."

"God knows I haven't been very good at saying the right things to you, but I'm trying here. There isn't a script to this. Be patient with me."

Fear began to cloud his eyes.

"You can't be gone for months and come back and say those things. Before I fell in love with you? Really, Jenner."

He raked his fingers through his hair. "I didn't leave, Lucy. You did. I've been searching. I've visited Pops half a dozen times. I've visited your old apartment that now has someone else living there. I've been to Henley's. Midge's. YOU left."

My hands flew up to my hips then to my temples. "You didn't want me. You said that many times. You said we were a fabrication. I was going to ruin your career." I wiped my tears and my snot with my hand.

Jenner's face hardened. "For God's sake, Lucy. What did you want me to tell a reporter? I was just as concerned about your credibility as mine. What would you have preferred I said?"

He had me flustered. I searched every inch of his face, looking for any sign of doubt. My memory didn't do him justice. His chest seemed broader, his eyes darker and he hadn't shaved. So, striking.

The sexual tension in the room steadily built. That electricity between us still sparked.

"I'm so scared." I cried silent tears that never made it down my cheeks because Jenner was suddenly beside me cupping my jaw as his thumbs erased the wetness.

"Don't be scared. Please, Lucy. Of all the emotions for you to feel, scared should be the last on your list."

I inhaled his breath. It had been so long. His father's vile words echoed through my brain.

"Your father," I whispered as my expression crumbled.

Jenner released my jaw and wrapped his palms around my cheeks. "No intelligent sentence should ever start with my father. Ever. He isn't worth the time or wasted energy."

"He told me I was trash. That I would never be welcomed into your family." My voice cracked. "I'm not trash."

Lifting my chin, he stared into the depth of my soul. "You aren't even close to trash. I'm trash too in his book because I don't do things his way. He means nothing to us."

"Jenner. I'm having his grandchild."

"And that, my dear, means I'm going to be a dad and you're going to be a mom—the best fucking mom in the world." He kissed the tip of my nose. "And we get the chance to do it so much better than our parents did."

This time when he bent down level with my bump...our bump... his knees cracked. His fingers inched my tank up, so he could kiss my slightly protruding belly.

"Wiilllllllllsuuuuun," he fake shouted, reminding me again of our Tom Hanks Castaway conversation. "Our little Wilson, Lucy. This little guy is going to be begging to get away from his helicopter mother and his rigid, wealth word talking father—by the time he reaches age of majority."

I giggled for the first time in months. "It could be a little gal."

"Dear God. If she has red hair and your sass, I'm screwed."

There was a certain way he said things that completely captivated me. As I looked down at him, happiness beamed through his eyes.

"Jen-ner," I whispered, my body responding to our proximity and to what I saw in his eyes.

His tongue peeked out between his lips indicative of a kiss to come. His lips brushed over the baby bump. Time and time again.

"What's that?" he asked the bump, then placed his ear flush with my belly.

He covered his open-mouthed gape.

"What?" I asked, smiling.

"Wilson said that his mother needs me to be inside of her."

I giggled. "Did he now?"

Jenner smiled that big, toothy smile that had caught my attention the first night I met him. The night in the club when I shouted if he'd have sex with me.

With his thumbs, he inched my sweats down over my hips. I covered myself, trying to hide my not so groomed private parts. "Jenner, I wasn't prepared for this."

He grinned. "I've not seen you in months. I've not tasted you. I've not been inside you. I don't care if Welcome to the jungle is blaring as your legs part."

I laughed.

"I want to make you come more than anything right now." His fingers slid through my wetness as my head fell back.

"You know, there's a bonus for you. No condom," I said into the air.

"That is a bonus," he said, nudging his nose back and forth over my bump as his hands slid around to grip my ass.

"I have two more questions before I surrender."

He rubbed over the exact spot he knew would make my knees go weak. I gripped his shoulders.

"Jenner. That makes it difficult to concentrate."

"I'm sorry. I'm listening," he whispered as he slid one finger inside me.

Flashbacks of our first night together flooded through my mind. Him making me come with his fingers before his phone rang. I wanted that again. Tonight. I wanted everything he had to give.

"That's complete and total bullshit. I'm not listening," he chuckled, stimulating me to the point that my legs trembled. "I just need to know that you're mine, Lucy. The rest we can handle together. You and I... we can handle anything."

There's something about the most pleasurable feeling in the world—something that makes you not care what your face looks like or what sounds you make. Where nothing around you makes sense. That's the moment I was lost in.

"Lay me down," I begged.

"I've been waiting months to hear you say that."

Time stopped—and nothing mattered but us as he snagged the quilt off the sofa, preparing a make-shift bed. I began to wiggle out of my sweat pants.

"No! Please, allow me."

Jenner fell to his knees eager to please as he removed my sweats and panties.

"Raise your arms."

I did. When my breast fell free of the tank, a familiar heaviness settled in them. As he massaged my breasts, now a little fuller than before, his fingers circled my nipples causing a sharp intake of breath—from both of us.

"They're tender," I panted.

He nodded as he lowered his mouth gently over my breast. My insides tingled as every sense came alive.

Everything. Me. Him. Us. The way our fingers and hands knew each other's bodies. It all fell right into place as every ounce of doubt fluttered away.

I came first around his finger, then he slid deliberately, slowly inside of me robbing me of breath.

"Am I hurting you?"

"No. I need you. I need you, Jenner. So much."

"Oh, Christ, Lucy. I need you too. Never. Never leave me again. Losing you would destroy me."

I arched my hips up to meet his tender thrusts. That same look I'd had earlier of getting lost in the moment—the inability to concentrate on anything but the feeling growing inside of me—was now evident on Jenner's face. I worked my hips, longing to please him but also as my own orgasm peaked.

"I love you, Lucy."

I couldn't respond. I wouldn't respond. Not lost in the emotion of this. I did love him. How many times had I cried in Ethan's arms over the past few months claiming my love for Jenner?

His mouth covered mine as he breathed his love into me. I inhaled every last bit. And as his thrusts quickened, his low moans echoed through the room and reverberated through my body. There it was—the look I wanted—the whites of his eye disappeared behind the fluttering of lids. His lips parted as the most pleasurable groan scraped up his throat. I don't remember feeling it the first time when I conceived, but

I felt every contraction, every spurt, and every seed of love. He rested next to me; his eyes skated over each inch of my face.

Between the front door slamming and Jenner bolting off of me, I grabbed a pillow unsure of what was happening. Ethan's eyes widened as he rounded the corner.

"What the hell?" Jenner ground out, trying to block me.

"Lucy?" Ethan questioned.

"This is not a good time, man."

"I'm not your man."

Ethan stepped closer and both Jenner's hands flew up to Ethan's chest.

I scrambled to my feet, covering myself with the quilt. "Ethan, what's wrong?" I stepped between them. I'd never seen any sort of snarl on Jenner's face—but one side of his lip pulled up.

"I called you several times. You didn't answer," Ethan explained.

"As you can see, we were preoccupied."

"Jenner, please." I swatted my hand at him. "Is something wrong, E?"

Ethan shoved his hands into his front jean pockets and looked down at the ground. "I just needed to know you were alright."

"As you can see, she is perfectly fine."

If looks could kill, Ethan would have murdered Jenner. I pushed Ethan back away from Jenner.

"I'm ok," I whispered. "I'm better than ok."

He nodded again. "I'm sorry. This is hard for me. He hurt you and that's not ok."

"Yes. He did. And I hurt him."

"You're sure about this?"

I smiled at him. "Yes. I am. And I love you for worrying, you mother hen."

He grinned and glanced back at Jenner.

"Do I have to like him?"

"That would help. Because I really need you in my life."

"Well, I don't want to like him today. I'll do better tomorrow."

Ethan gave me a tight-lipped grin, then winked as he stepped past me and walked right back out the door almost as suddenly as he came.

"Do you want to tell me what that's about?" Jenner asked, still buck ass naked.

I giggled when I saw him standing there.

"I'm not amused, Lucy."

"Ethan saw you naked, Jenner. Surely you think that is a little funny."

His eyes fell to his front side as a lopsided grin replaced his scowl. "It would have been nice if he'd have barged in before I came."

I glanced down at him and then bit my bottom lip.

Jenner tilted his head to the side and his eyelids lowered about half way. As he made his way toward me, blood began to make its way back into his dick.

"Once. That's all I need to hear it. Tell me I don't need to worry about Ethan. Tell me that you are mine, Lucy, without a reasonable doubt."

With his thumb, he freed my lip from my teeth.

"You don't need to worry about anyone. Ever. I love you, Jenner. I love *you*."

Jenner's entire expression lit as he swept me off my feet. "Point me in the direction of our bedroom."

"Our bedroom?"

"Yep. If I'm yo baby daddy, then I'm shacking up with you too."

I pointed to my bedroom. "Don't ever talk like that again," I giggled.

As he strolled through the door, he smiled. "I know we've never really been out on a date—at least officially. Would it be forward of me to ask you out on a date?"

With the utmost gentleness, he laid me on the bed.

"I'm sorry. No dating. I'm just using you for sex. You ok with that?" I teased.

His eyes danced with laughter. "As long as it's once a day for as long as we both shall live, I have no problem."

"Or longer."

Jenner yanked the comforter up, covering our heads, and even though I knew what was coming...for a moment, he held me as close as he could get me.

"Lucy?"

"Yeah?"

"I know I hurt you. I'm going to spend the rest of forever making up for that. I'm right here for the entire world to see that I'm yours. I lived in this perfect little world that my father created for me, never realizing that person wasn't me…that it was his version of me. I don't like that person. I don't like the way that person treated you and I'd like the chance to rewrite our ending."

Tears filled my eyes and immediately brimmed over.

"If that ending includes the words happily ever after, then I'm in."

Jenner kissed away the tears that left my eyes.

My heart was full…no…not full—overflowing. For the first time in my life, I felt wanted and loved. Pops had brought me back to life when I was little, but Jenner made me feel alive. Together, we would create a life that I might not have originally thought I wanted but needed more than I could ever know.

EPILOGUE

FIVE YEARS LATER

"Jenner!" Lucy yelled.

"Daddy, Mommy needs you."

"Yep, I heard her buddy. We better go. Hop on."

Wilson jumped off the tractor onto my back. First harvest was underway, and I'd finally gotten the hang of it. Staying on the farm was the best decision we'd ever made.

Walking through the field, Wilson held tightly to my neck as we headed to the house. Lucy stood on the big wrap around porch with her swollen belly protruding against her sundress. An uncontrollable smiled plastered across my face. She was as beautiful today as the day I found her in that bar.

"How was the city?" I asked not missing it even a little bit. But, my girl still loved it.

"Alive and well. The foundation got a new federal grant. We've been approved to go into some of the inner city pre-schools."

Wilson slid off my back and ran to his mother. She bent down to his level throwing him her undivided attention.

"You, mister, are dirty." She pinched his nose then put her thumb between her index and middle finger.

"Mommy, give me my nose," he laughed.

"You give me a kiss and you get your nose."

Wilson leaned in kissing her lips.

"Oh my goodness. You're lips are sticky," she said wiping her mouth with the back of her hand.

"Daddy and I cracked open a watermelon in the field."

"Did you now?"

"Yep. Daddy said that was what Pops used to do."

Her eyes batted repeatedly and I knew she fought tears.

Pops had passed not long after Wilson was born but Lucy and I tried to remind him of who Pops was and the things he loved. Today, it was watermelon.

"Pops loved watermelon especially on a hot day like this. Why don't you go wash the sticky from your face and hands?"

Wilson ran inside and it was my turn to greet my bride.

"I'm proud of you with the preschool thing. That's awesome."

I pressed one hand against her belly while the other wrapped around the back of her neck pulling her in for a kiss. God made one set of lips that were made for mine and they were Lucy's.

"You taste like watermelon," she whispered.

"I'll give you one guess what I'd like to taste."

"Jenner," she shushed me glancing at the door Wilson had gone through.

"I'm not joking. Ethan and Claire will be here around 7 tonight to take Wilson."

"What for?"

"So I can violate his mother without him being in the same house. I don't want to be shushed during sex. I don't want you to have to be reserved. So, they are helping me out."

Lucy shook her head as blood seeped into her cheeks.

"And Ethan has agreed to this?"

I shrugged. "He agreed to come and get Wilson."

"You didn't tell him why," she laughed. "After five years, you're still afraid of him, aren't you?"

A lopsided grin blew over my face. "Maybe."

She swatted her hand at me. "Go wash up."

"Oh, you can tell me what to do right now but come seven o'clock,

Judge Weber is in the house. Court will be in session," I threatened. Her entire body shuddered with my words and I smiled.

ACKNOWLEDGEMENTS

BOOK 10!!! Thank you so much to the readers who support me. I love creating this world in my head then getting it on paper. You all are the reason I write. The author world continues to grow—it seems like daily and I appreciate that you chose my book to read. From the bottom of my heart, I thank you.

MCM—Megan, Clista and Madison—always. Lisa and Tera—much love from Kansas. Amber—Best ARC reader/Best mom. Ketty—you keep it real and I thank you. Sandra and Tracy (you two go hand in hand) Love!! Elaine and Janet—Loyal forever. Vanessa—Thank you. The girls that still hang—Jazzy J, Riza, Heather, Laura... thank you! BB McNeil—thank you!

A special shout out to Love Affair with Fiction and Jill for her help. The indie Bookshelf and Beth for her unwavering support. The Book Bistro! There are so many blogs!! Jenny at TotallyBooked Eye Candy (Carrie!), Book Obsessed and Kinky Girls! There are 1000 blogs and and I thank each of you that shared me!

My gym wives and beast. My besties—Susy-q, Kat, Deanna, Lorraine. All provide great reading material. My job—you peeps know who you are. I couldn't write some of this stuff without the...knowledge and experience. ☺

My mom and my dad—who I want to make proud every day! Even given the sauciness of what I write—they still brag about their daughter! I love you!

K-dawg, B-pup and Z-man...thank you for this wonderful journey of life. Thank you for making me laugh. I love you. Here we go...

Go Cubs! Go Jayhawks! Go Ducks!

K, B, Z...1

Made in the USA
Monee, IL
19 December 2020

54069760R00111